THE AMERICAN COLLECTION 10: COMPROMISING LOVE

Dixie Lynn Dwyer

LOVEXTREME FOREVER

Siren Publishing, Inc.
www.SirenPublishing.com

A SIREN PUBLISHING BOOK
IMPRINT: LoveXtreme Forever

THE AMERICAN SOLDIER COLLECTION 10: COMPROMISING
LOVE
Copyright © 2015 by Dixie Lynn Dwyer

ISBN: 978-1-63258-948-4

First Printing: February 2015

Cover design by Les Byerley
All art and logo copyright © 2015 by Siren Publishing, Inc.

Printed in the U.S.A.

PUBLISHER
Siren Publishing, Inc.
www.SirenPublishing.com

DEDICATION

Dear readers,

Thank you for purchasing this legal copy of Compromising Love.

When many people think of their homes, their bedrooms, they think of security, comfort, and peace of mind. But Aspen Brooks is alone in her penthouse, night after night waking in terror caused by fear from her past. She shares this with no one, not even her brother or her closest friend. She doesn't want to feel vulnerable, weak, or to give in to the label of "victim."

She is not the only one who has placed armor over her heart, her soul, in order to remain battle ready. She even engages in business dealings close to where the person responsible for her fears conducts his own business. The Russian Mafia is not exactly an organization to challenge. But she has her own ways of seeking revenge that eventually lands her in a heap of trouble.

Fate has a way of exposing the truth, and bringing together those scarred souls and making them heal, and eventually be free. Revenge is a very deep, controlling emotion that easily becomes an obsession. That obsession could cause Aspen to lose everything, including the ones who penetrate her armored heart.

May you enjoy Aspen's journey.

Happy reading.

Hugs!

~Dixie~

THE AMERICAN SOLDIER COLLECTION 10: COMPROMISING LOVE

DIXIE LYNN DWYER

Prologue

Storm Jones awoke in a cold sweat, the sound of screams filling his dreams once again. Sleepless nights were customary for any soldier who experienced war in their lives. For any man who conducted crimes or committed murder, even if only by giving an order from their command. He'd experienced it all. But nothing. Not the battles he fought to defend and protect his company and his team, nor the gruesome acts of violence he witnessed others commit on the innocent, stood out like that one night on US soil.

He ran his hand over the scruff on his face as he sat on the side of the bed calming his breathing. He stood up and made his nightly journey to the kitchen, being sure to walk with light feet and not wake his roommates, his team members.

But he knew they heard him. Night after night, hours of sleeplessness plagued them, for they shared the same nightmares, the same feelings of fear at what could have gone so terribly wrong if they'd taken thirty seconds longer to get to the scene.

When Storm entered the kitchen, there was Zin.

He shouldn't have been surprised to see him there, too. He gave a nod to his friend, his brother-in-arms and the best sniper shot Storm ever came across in his sixteen-year military career.

Zin poured him a glass of water and pushed it across the large granite island in the modern kitchen. They were surrounded by black granite, stainless steel, and black custom cabinetry. They all agreed that they liked the darker colors, the sleek appearance of a modern, high-class penthouse. It was far from the places they'd stayed while serving in the military and even the shit holes each of them grew up in. But really, all that steel, stone, and blackness represented so much more, like each of their personalities.

"Back to Chicago for the next few weeks. I hate leaving Salvation. I like it here," Zin said as he took a sip from his glass of water, never looking at Storm. They didn't talk about emotions, about the fears they had. None of them did. Not him, not Zin, Winter, Weston, or York. They had desires, dreams that grew because of what they'd witnessed around them, but none seemed to fit into their feelings of being complete, except for her.

He cleared his mind best he could. He had to keep his focus on the businesses and the direction they wanted to go in.

"It looks that way, but it's temporary. We need to show our faces or God knows what these employees of ours will do to fuck things up," Storm replied.

"I know. It's not that I don't like Chicago. It can be a fun city with the right people. But Salvation is different. Hanging out at the end of the week at Casper's with some of our buddies makes me feel normal."

"Normal? What's not fucking normal about our lives?" Storm asked and then leaned back in the chair and took a sip of water from his own glass.

"Being fucking billionaires. Running both types of businesses and trying to act like we're legit when really we're not. We've been saying that we want out. That we want to be free from the mob, yet here we fucking go again."

"What? We're doing what we need to survive. None of us want to truly give up the power, the connections and contacts we have out there. We're pretty fucking powerful, and we're not killing people or committing murder for money, or running prostitution rings. We're collecting on money, money we helped these businesses acquire. We can't just pass that up. It's not how this works and you know it."

"I know that. Nicolai likes that we're still involved. But you know he could take over our share of this shit. We could just take him up on his offer of being silent partners."

"Like that would last long? I've known Nicolai longer than any of you. It's his way of squeezing us out nicely because of our relationship."

"Which is exactly what, Storm? What is the deep connection between you and Nicolai?"

Storm placed the glass down and locked gazes with Zin.

"We've known one another a very long time. There are things that happened before I entered the service. Things I don't need to look back on but tied me to Nicolai in a way that can't be severed. Let's focus on what we need to do. With Sotoro fucking around behind our backs and God knows who else he brought in to help take over our businesses, I think we have greater concerns right now."

I can't tell him or the others about the blood we share. The connection deeper than a business relationship.

"Yeah, like securing our company Pro-Tech Industries and trying to eliminate the competition of Sparks Industries."

Storm chuckled. "You know Gary Sparks will be moving on soon enough. He's playing a little hardball right now with the numbers and doesn't realize that we haven't even begun negotiations. He'll come through."

"He's also Dmitri's connection with that new multimillion-dollar construction job here in Texas. Do you think Dmitri even has a chance of landing that job with Andrei Renoke all over that?"

Storm felt his anger rise. He hated Andrei Renoke and his team of Russian and Slavic mobsters with a passion. He couldn't do anything about it. Storm and his team did business in Texas and in Chicago, and the different families that ruled the territories had the respect and the acceptance of Nicolai Merkovicz, the head of all of it. But if Dmitri landed the job, then Pro-Tech Industries would get the contracts for all the security jobs, including the work for their friends' company, Liberty Construction and Development. Asher, Avery, Beau, Blade, and Cason were some of their closest friends and colleagues now living in Pearl.

"In all honesty, I don't know if Dmitri has a chance. Winter's connections believe that Andrei's got it wrapped up. We'll know soon enough."

Zin ran the tip of his finger over the empty water glass.

"Have you heard from Porter?"

Storm took a deep breath and released it. Porter was Aspen's brother and a close friend of theirs from the military. Zin worried about Aspen. He and the rest of the team had talked about offering her a job retraining their employees that were in charge of evaluating potential clients searching for missing people. One case nearly backfired and cost a woman's life when her ex hired their company. If better, more in-depth questions were asked, then they wouldn't have had to send in Porter and his team to help save the woman's life.

"He's supposed to touch base tomorrow."

"It is tomorrow," Zin said and then smirked before he stood up and walked his glass to the sink. "I'm going to try and get a little more rest."

Storm nodded his head and watched Zin leave the room.

His men were good men. They were strong, resourceful, loyal, and they all wanted the same thing, yet knew they could never have her.

As their commander, he'd had access to their personal files back in the military. He'd picked them by their experiences, their abilities, and their survival instincts. They were so much like him in many ways, and their connections, their common grounds brought them closer than any of them expected.

Each of them—Winter, Weston, Zin, and York—had troubled pasts as teens who came from broken homes and poverty.

They entered the military for a way out of their shitty homelives and as a last resort to surviving life. They each had a story to tell. They were so much like him and the family he came from.

Storm swallowed hard. He entered the military as an escape from his responsibilities and knowing that he wanted his own future, his own dreams and accomplishments, and not one attached to a name. But so much had changed. All the years he and his team served doing all those special operations and risking their lives didn't leave them the security and the monetary cushion they all deserved for all they did. Instead it left them on their asses with nowhere to live, no better way of life, and ultimately him making a decision to save not only himself but also his team, his family.

Truth was, they had all been so used to taking orders and completing dangerous missions, and so filled with anger and a need for that adrenaline rush they felt whenever they were in the midst of a war, a battle, or gunfire, that working for Nicolai felt right. Storm had a knack for business as did Winter and Weston. Zin and York were great at organizing, planning, working those numbers, and putting on the pressure to get a response. Together they were feared, and eventually in two years' time they became part of an organization Storm had joined the military to get away from.

He looked around the room at all the upscale items and décor. He preferred their house in Salvation on the ranch way outside the city and twenty minutes from Casper's. Zin was right. This was where they felt most normal. But they weren't *normal*. They were made men. They'd made the decision when faced with surviving civilian life, and that decision had its positives and its negatives.

They were trying so hard to go legit, but it seemed like they were never going to be able to get out of the Russian Mafia. Their connections and their abilities lay deep. The assets they now had were worth way more than any monetary value. They couldn't make Aspen be part of this type of life. She would never be free. She would immediately be placed in danger as their enemies constantly searched for ways to penetrate their empire.

No, they had to stay clear of Aspen. Keeping her safe, watching over her as Porter asked when he was away on business or working on their estate in Tranquility, was as close as they could get to her. Offering her a job retraining their employees was really a ploy by Porter to keep her out of Chicago and away from threats from her past. The damn woman was stubborn, but also the only woman Storm would ever love. The only woman his team would ever want. But they had to keep that love, that desire, a secret. It was the only way to keep her alive.

Chapter 1

Aspen Brooks crossed her legs and watched Clarence Cartwright's eyes zero in on her body. She wanted this deal to go through for so many reasons. Initially revenge had ruled her mind. Knowing who some of the players were and risking her life, her soul, to get the information she wanted hadn't even fazed her. She was so damn hollow inside and there wasn't a thing she could do about it. That saying that time heals all wounds was a load of bullshit when it came to her and her experience. No, she wasn't healable.

This was the third damn meeting with this man, a multimillionaire who wanted to build a major business complex in Texas that would eventually expand over thousands of acres of prime land. If successful, which she truly thought he would be without a doubt, he would be worth billions.

"I'm impressed with the work you've done with these numbers, Aspen. Your concepts and Dmitri's are so much better than anything I've personally come up with in design," Clarence said as he looked over the portfolio and her own personal ideas she felt he would be impressed with. Clarence leaned forward and looked her over.

She was dressed a little less conservatively in her designer knee-length, beige skirt that hugged her shapely figure and the camisole in pale yellow that showed off a bit of cleavage. Her designer bangle bracelets were in great contrast to the small heart of tiny diamonds that her brother had brought her right before he left for the military. She was only a kid, barely a teenager, but she cherished it.

Many people asked her why she wore such a plain, minuscule heart when she could afford one loaded with huge diamonds. They didn't understand her. The wealth and reputation she'd established in business was her way of surviving.

"Are you certain that I can't interest you in coming to work for me? We would be good together, Aspen." He held her gaze with hunger in his eyes. She knew that look and just like all the others, it did nothing for her. There were only a handful of men that made her body, and her emotions react to them. They were five men she could never have because they didn't share the same feelings and thought of her like a baby sister.

She smiled and ran her hand across the pictures on the table, picking one up and looking it over.

"I'll think about it, Clarence. You do know how much I like Texas. I prefer it over any other place."

He looked her over and leaned back in his chair.

"I've often wondered why it is you work for a man like Dmitri. You've established your own reputation in the business world. You can basically name your price and land any job you want in most major cities." She raised one eyebrow up at him, surprised by his question.

He was dressed casually with a white button-down shirt and khaki pants. They were out on his yacht and miles from shore. He quickly added as he leaned forward in his chair, "Don't get me wrong. I like Dmitri. I understand what I'm getting involved with if I choose to use his company and all his connections. It's the same with Andrei Renoke."

"Oh, no it isn't. Renoke will weasel his way into taking over your project. At first he'll start with suggestions, ideas that you'll pay for, and then he'll begin asking for a cut, a partnership in building this enterprise of yours. Dmitri doesn't want to take your limelight. Dmitri wants to ensure his companies and employees have work, and bring in income, keeping him and his associates at the top of the list of the best. They're your hired help. You remain in charge, at the center of it all, and everything remains Clarence Cartwright's."

He gave a small smile. "I suppose you know who Dmitri would like to use in establishing the first building, the security and main offices of the project."

"Of course. The information about the companies is right here." She reached for the folder and opened up the one on Pro-Tech Industries and then the one on Liberty Construction and Development.

"These are the top contenders for the job. I can personally vouch for both of them. You won't find a better, fairer priced security firm and construction development company around."

He looked at the documents though she knew he'd already done his research.

"Renoke's workers are immigrants trying to make it in this country after fleeing some pretty devastating conditions," he told her. She knew that Cartwright was a patriotic man. A true Texan through and through.

"Liberty Construction and Development and Pro-Tech Industries, employ retired and even disabled military veterans and their families. There are men and women who have risked their lives to keep our country safe and secure. They're American citizens surviving and providing for their families and loved ones. But, the choice is yours, Clarence," she told him and he held her gaze then gave a small smile.

"I'll need to look these over and compare to Renoke's offer. I'll get back to you. I'll have my secretary call to set up another meeting soon."

She nodded her head.

"You have my personal cell phone number, Clarence. Call me. I want you to understand what I'm offering. Dmitri is offering that personal touch, the traditional handshake relationship that has been the start of thousands, if not millions, of successful business deals since the establishment of this great country of ours."

He stood up and so did she. Clarence reached out and she shook his hand. He held it a little longer than a handshake should be.

"I'll hold you to that, darling, and that personal touch. The commitment of a true relationship so that my dream can become a reality."

"The ball is in your court, sir. I look forward to hearing back from you soon."

He released her hand and she bent down to grab her purse.

"You'll stay for some lunch, won't ya?" he asked then proceeded to tell her about the lobsters and the items the chef was preparing. Clarence was a decent-looking man, a bit of extra pounds around his center but still very macho and manly, as a cowboy should be. But again, she felt no attraction. Not even enough to fake a roll in the hay, and she never shit where she ate.

"Of course I can. That's so kind of you to offer." He guided her toward the stairs, his hand at her lower back. The convincing wasn't done quite yet. Now she had to seal the deal with casual conversation, a personal touch beyond the meeting room, and hopefully a new business venture would begin. After all, the point of taking on this job for Dmitri was all part of the revenge she sought.

She could ensure that Pro-Tech Industries, Storm and his team's business, landed this job along with Dmitri's construction company and not Renoke's.

Andrei Renoke was a slimy, Russian mobster, and a man partially responsible for her abduction and near death. She was going to get him where it would hurt the most. His wallet. If he threatened her, so be it. She had no fear. No recollection of how she was rescued. But she remembered the pain, the broken bones, and being dragged over concrete to an awaiting cargo ship headed to some third world country. Andrei Renoke, a man responsible for running a sex slave business, would pay big-time. Not only for what she went through, but also for all those innocent women who never made it out alive. Revenge was a powerful emotion indeed.

* * * *

"Of course I don't like any of the shit I'm hearing. But what do we do? Andrei's a ruthless businessman. He's had his claws in Cartwright for years just waiting on this opportunity. There's plenty of other work out there," Winter said to Weston.

"But this is fucking huge. It's thousands of acres of land to develop. It's near Salvation, Tranquility, and Casper's. This could give us the opportunity to focus solely on this job and retire. Get the fuck out of this business," Weston told him.

"It's not that easy. Yes, this could be the opportunity to start easing further away from the mob connections in a sense. We could let Nicolai take over our share and step down. But I think the opposite might happen," Storm added.

"What do you mean?" Weston asked.

"He means that if Dmitri lands this job, it's going to piss off a lot of major people. This could cause all of us nothing but problems. Renoke, Demyan, and Iakov will all suffer financial loss and lose a lot of power and authority in the eyes of the top bosses. We'll gain more respect, and it will be looked at as a strategic move to monopolize Texas and Chicago. We're staking a deeper claim in the mob," Zin stated.

"Like that's so fucking bad? We pretty much established that these are our lives now. We're made men. We are doing more than a billion a year in revenue, and if by some miracle we get this, we're in the deepest we can be. There'll be no going back. There'll be no becoming regular civilian businessmen. We're going to need our own security details and personal bodyguards," York said.

Everyone remained quiet a moment.

"What else do we have? We know nothing better than this business. We'll be helping thousands of military families find steady work for years, because that's how long this project will take. This is serious American money to be made," Weston added.

"But what about Aspen?" Zin asked.

Winter took a deep breath and released it. "You know the answer to that. We all fucking do," he said in annoyance. They all wanted her. Had watched over her and hoped to keep her as far away from trouble as possible, yet she seemed to wind up pretty damn close to it. Working for Dmitri, a made man and one of the major bosses in Chicago, wasn't what her brother Porter or any of them had wanted. But she was great at business. She was a workaholic, a woman running from her past, her fears, and dealing with it in the best way she knew how to. How badly Winter would love to have her. To share her with the rest of the team. But that would put her in the ultimate danger, and she'd survived death once. She wouldn't survive this time.

"I'd give it all up for her," Zin added.

"But that isn't how this works, Zin. We're stuck. We made our beds. We have to live with the decisions we made when we returned from the service and realized there was nothing here for us. No parades, no financial backing, nothing but shitty pay, food stamps, and a fate similar if not worse than what we all ran from and entered the service to get away from as teens," Storm told them.

"He's right. She suffered enough. We can't expose Aspen to the life like ours. We have to hide our feelings. So whatever happens with this deal, we accept it and do our jobs. We could never ask her to expose herself to the dangers of being the lover to five made men. Her freedom, her own dreams and achievements, would be taken from her and she would feel more like a prisoner again than a woman set free. Discussion over," Winter said, and they all somberly agreed.

* * * *

Aspen Brooks knew she shouldn't have had that third glass of wine. Now, feeling tipsy, she stood by the wall in the dining room at the banquet hall and stared at Storm Jones's lips. The man was freaking mysterious. He made every part of her body stand at attention and so did the rest of his team. Winter, Weston, York, and Zin were dangerous men for many reasons. But the most intimidating thing for her was that they were very good friends with her brother Porter.

Navy SEALs, now retired, Storm and his crew weren't exactly model citizens. No, their ties to the Russian mob and the illegal and legal businesses they owned and operated brought their team billions in revenue. But she wasn't interested in their money. Hell, unlike most women who flocked around these men trying to land them, Aspen had her own money, her own achievements, and was considered pretty darn ruthless in her own ways. She was a hard-ass, yet approachable, easy to get along with as long as people followed her orders.

Her jobs ranged from reorganizing and training employees at high-end companies, to making their sales departments run more efficiently, to evaluating businesses that needed to be revamped. More recently she was getting into negotiating large money deals between some of the most ruthless, notorious billionaires of the United States, never mind the world. Yeah, she was involved with a lot of things. Things that, if her brother Porter found out, would get her in serious trouble. But truth was, some of the contacts she'd made because of Porter and Storm looked to her for advice. They sought her out and eventually she landed some private gigs that had her rolling in the money and deciding if it were time to settle down somewhere and just live a normal life. But she wasn't normal. Hadn't been normal since she was a teen and before she had been abducted.

She cleared her mind and listened to Storm's voice as he spoke. She nodded her head to the others as if she were totally paying attention to their business conversation. She knew Storm was hinting about needing some assistance at his company Pro-Tech Industries with retraining employees, but she wasn't sure she was interested. Besides, she was already helping them without them knowing by trying to land this business deal with Dmitri. God, if Porter or Storm and the crew found out what kind of business dealings she had been involved in lately, there would be hell to pay.

Was she a glutton for punishment though? She would love to feel anything from Storm, Winter, Weston, York or even Zin. Although in her fantasies she would love a good spanking by them. That would surely make her orgasm like a woman should be able to.

But they didn't know what she knew about Andrei or about them for that matter. They tried to hide the culprits behind her abduction from her. But it didn't take long to realize it had been Andrei Renoke. Nor did it take long, well five years exactly, to find out about her family ties to the Mafia. But that was a different story entirely, and apparently one relationship severed years ago, when her mother was still alive.

Either way, she was more alone now than she'd ever felt before. It was crazy, but she wasn't quite finding that closure she was searching for even though she was pretty sure she'd landed that construction deal for Dmitri.

She was a free agent really. Could basically take on any jobs she wanted to. It would be great to help out Storm, Winter, Zin, Weston, and York with improving their business and revamping their employees training regimen. She looked at Storm again. Her heart felt as if it beat a little faster. He hadn't even looked her body over or showed any interest whatsoever. Meanwhile she lusted for him. For any of his team of gods to notice her, never mind make a move.

She didn't think she could handle being in the same office building as Storm, Winter, Weston, York, and Zin, some of the sexiest, most desirable men around. She was such a loser, holding out for the chance that they could give her the orgasm of her dreams. No other man had been successful in making her feel anything. She was a lost cause in that department.

Lately, she found herself assisting with less high-profile cases and more intimate businesses. Negotiating private contracts amongst high-profile individuals was by accident, but quite lucrative.

Although half the men she assisted with business dealings wanted to land her as their woman or at minimal their lover, she never entertained their advances. She had her own hang-ups and insecurities she hid behind her designer attire, top-line fashions, and exotic vacations with fellow single friends. She was independent, yet yearned for male company she could rely on and trust. But trust was something that seemed unobtainable as far as she was concerned.

So why was she staring so intently at Storm and noticing every tiny detail about him? The small scar by his right eye, barely noticeable. The way he crossed his arms in front of his sexy, muscular chest when he was truly focusing on the person's conversation he was engaged in. His blond hair, cut to perfection, and his designer dress shirt and tie he wore spoke volumes about his personality and the fact the man had style and money. He was a bad boy, capable of things she didn't even want to think about and knew too well that he was capable of accomplishing.

She should fear him and his buddies, for the simple fact that they had connections to people like Andrei as well as other higher-ups. She knew they weren't the kind of men to gain money from sex slave businesses, prostitution, guns, and drugs. Or at least she didn't think them capable of such criminal activity.

Why women found gangsters, made men, so sexy and appealing she wasn't certain. Maybe it was the mystery, the darkness about them and their capabilities. Add in that Storm and his crew were military men and hell yeah, she found it all sexy. It aroused her, interested her as she took a sip from her glass of wine and forced her eyes to move on to something else and maintain the distance she needed for her sanity.

"Aspen, won't you consider helping Storm out with his business? You're so good at revamping and training employees on the subject of security measures. You would be an asset to the business," John Brothers said and then smiled at her.

"I'm not sure I'm right for the position." She glanced at Storm, who watched her lips and then eyed her over. It'd only taken him an hour to actually check her out. She was wearing a pretty sexy dress, too. The man should totally be taking advantage of their close proximity. But he wasn't because he wasn't interested.

She needed some fresh air, some distance from him and his buddies. She couldn't think straight and the wine was messing with her head.

As she began to excuse herself, she felt the hand on her hip and then a body press against her back.

"Have you convinced her to help us and accept the position?" Winter asked from behind her. She closed her eyes and absorbed the feel of his thick, hard hand on her waist and his large presence behind her. She didn't even have to turn to feel the attraction to the man. Blond hair, hazel eyes, and a firm expression he was known for. His name suited him well. He always looked so complex and in turmoil. His eyes were filled with emotion and his expressions just as dark and intriguing. So badly she wanted to run her palms along his cheeks, turn those frowns and concerns into smiles of pleasure. But who was she? She didn't have the capabilities to do such things. She was fucked up in her own ways. No one could touch her so deeply, nor could she ever touch someone's heart with such depth either.

She was so affected by these men. Each of them, yet she could never entertain that attraction. It would be disastrous.

She stepped from his hold and smiled.

"Sorry, Winter, I just don't think it would work out. Besides, I'm currently working on too many other projects to even consider this opportunity with you. I can always refer you to someone else who would be suitable for the position if you needed." She hated to offer anyone else to them. She could recommend Clare, Monique, or even Stella, but then she got this instant jealous feeling just thinking that one of the men could hook up with those women.

She could only imagine Zin, York, or Weston bending Stella over one of their desks and having their way with her. She cringed and pulled away.

Weston, York, and Zin were a wild bunch, too. She heard they all shared women at one time or another because the men were so close.

Aspen had to admit that not only the thought of sharing them excited her, but more importantly the thought of experiencing such a deep bond of trust like that had to be mind-blowing. As a matter of fact, she was more intrigued and attracted to know that these men shared such a deep, unbreakable bond. She hadn't had such a relationship with anyone ever. She loved her brother Porter, but there seemed to be some sort of invisible barrier between them, too. Maybe she wasn't the type of person someone could love?

Sure, she would risk her life for Porter. She would do whatever he asked of her, but the depth of their bond just wasn't as intense or pronounced as the bond these five men shared. It scared her. Yet it intrigued her.

"You should reconsider. The package deal we're offering is more than competitive, Aspen. It's insane for you not to accept it," Winter added, eyeing her body over then focusing on her lips.

She adjusted her stance and felt her unsteady movement before Storm took her arm to steady her.

She pulled away and cleared her throat.

"Maybe you should sit down a few minutes?" Storm suggested in that tone of his that instantly got under her skin. Those dark eyes alone could do her in.

"I don't think so. I just need some fresh air. If you'll please excuse me." She turned to walk toward the hallway that led to a balcony that overlooked the city. She had been in this penthouse before for a more intimate affair and business deal only a month or so earlier. It was an impressive setup.

She thought about Winter and Storm as she entered the balcony, closing the door behind her.

It was dark out here but the cool night air caressed against her heated skin, relieving some of the warmth. She wished it could also deflate her hardened nipples and aroused state, but no such luck. Why she continued to torture herself she didn't know. She turned down offers of sex and casual relationships with men because none of them came close to the effect Storm, Winter, Zin, Weston, and York caused within her. Maybe she was just using her crush on them as a defense mechanism to resist her needs and desires for safety and comfort. She knew damn well that in their arms, any of their arms, she would feel safest. It was so crazy. Meanwhile, never had any of them hugged her long enough to prove such capabilities. It was becoming pretty damn obvious that she'd created this image of them in her head as protectors. Perhaps it stemmed from them being retired military men? Navy SEALs specifically was a definite turn-on. Then there were their connections to the Russian Mafia, their ability and charismatic personalities that could land any piece of ass they wanted or directed their attention to, and yeah, she found it all sexy.

Fuck, that pissed her off. Just thinking of other women having sex with them, touching those muscular bodies she knew were to die for.

She took a deep breath and released it.

Get them out of your head. This isn't doing you any good.

She heard the door to the balcony open and thought for sure that Winter or Storm would be there. How would she hide her hardened nipples? Her flushed cheeks and the way the cream coated her thighs? But as she glanced over her shoulder, she saw Weston and York.

Two of the five men she was trying so hard to keep a distance from.

"We thought we saw you come out here. How are you feeling, Aspen?" Weston asked. Weston Galloway. A prize fighter and master in martial arts, retired Navy SEAL, accounting major, business entrepreneur, the man—just like his buddies—was one major, sought-after bachelor in the Chicago and Texas areas.

"I'm feeling great, and you?" she asked, hearing the attitude in her tone. Weston's eyes widened at her reply while York Reiss and his amazingly sexy hazel eyes stared at her then the cleavage in her dress.

"You seem a bit out of sorts tonight, Aspen. Anything we can do to help ease your mind?" York asked then reached over and moved her hair off her shoulder before he caressed his thumb and forefinger against her earlobe.

"Out of sorts? Hmm…I don't think so. I was just getting some fresh air before I called it a night and headed out of here. How about you two? Any plans for the rest of the night with any of the entertainment John has prancing around the penthouse this evening?" she asked, referring to the single bimbo women John always had attend these events in case any of the businessmen he invited were looking for free sex.

It kind of annoyed her, but at least she didn't come across as one of those women available for a sexual fling. She'd established years ago that she was not easy. In fact, her sex life was considered so secretive that there had been bets as to who could land her in the sack and as their woman. She had gotten entirely fed up with the flirtatious actions of men she had to deal with on a regular basis that she called in a friend to pretend that he was her lover. It worked and everyone backed off.

But Jester eventually took a job in Texas for work.

"We're not interested in the 'entertainment,' Aspen. We came here tonight because we knew that you were attending," York told her. She shot her head up to look at him.

Weston quickly added, "We wanted to offer you the business position with our company in Texas and perhaps if things worked out you could assist here in Chicago next. You're perfect for the job and certainly could get our employees trained accordingly." She felt disappointed and didn't know why. It wasn't like she lusted for these men, yet she had all the signs of someone with a crush. But not them. Not a bunch of men involved with things she should be intimidated by. Besides, it seemed their agenda kept coming back to keeping her out of Chicago. She knew why. They didn't know that she knew why, but still, it pissed her off. How badly she would love to hear one of them, if not all of them, say they wanted her with them.

But that wasn't the case. She lived for danger. She almost felt numb to pain and she knew it stemmed from her past.

"I really don't think I have the time right now to help you out. The offer was more than generous, and I would love to assist, but I'm in the middle of something major right now that has all my time wrapped up."

"Would you at least think about it for the next few weeks? Maybe give us a definite answer in a month? We have some things we're working on, too, right now and it would be better if you started after the summer," Weston said and then caressed her hand and brought it up to his lips. He kissed the top, and her heart skipped a beat as she locked gazes with his green eyes.

"Please? For us?" York added as he caressed her hair off her shoulder.

It was too much, having two men touch her at the same time. Although every nerve in her body knew their innocent touches were anything but innocent, she needed to maintain her composure and ensure these men couldn't get through the walls she built so strong.

"I'll let you know in a month or so."

They both smiled.

"Excellent. We'll let Storm, Winter, and Zin know."

Then they heard the door open and Zin walked out. He smiled and looked her over appreciatively, and she was glad she wore the slim-fitting black dress that accentuated her figure. Why she wanted them to desire her she really didn't know, especially when she would never allow them to know how she felt about them. Not that it mattered. These men didn't feel the same desire for her.

"Aspen, are they trying to change your mind about the job opportunity?" he asked, approaching and giving her a kiss on her cheek. She felt claustrophobic even though she was outside on the balcony.

"We should head back inside," she said when Zin stopped her by taking her hand. She nearly lost her footing and wound up against his chest. They stared at one another. He towered over her as did the others.

He held her gaze, and she swore he was going to kiss her, but then he stepped back. He turned from her, making her feel like shit. As if she weren't good enough, not even for a one-night stand. Or perhaps he thought of her as a sister because of Porter. After all Porter had to have told them that she had been abducted years ago. It was probably why they acted like overprotective brothers. As soldiers they put the needs of women and children first. Too bad they didn't know exactly what her needs were. Or maybe it was too bad she couldn't tell them and let them try to ease her fears and her resistance to physically connecting to another human being in a more intimate way. They knew she had hang-ups. In fact, they knew more than most.

"Be careful. Are you getting a ride home with someone?" Weston asked, sounding fatherly.

She shrugged her shoulders. "The night is still young," she said with attitude and opened the door and exited the balcony. She thought she heard cursing, but the sound of laughter as some drunk woman was lifted up over a guy's shoulder before they headed down the hallway to the bedrooms blocked out any other sounds.

Tonight, just like all the other nights the past four years, she would go home alone, and sleep in a bed scared, with the lights on. This was her future, the torture she continued to experience night after night. The nightmares ruled her mind and no one could help her get past them. No one.

She put on her game face and headed into the main room. Gary Sparks spotted her, and his eyes brightened, and he stopped talking to his friends to get to her.

"Aspen, I finally caught you alone. Can we talk about the meeting this week?" She didn't want to but at least the business dealings would take her mind off of the balcony scene.

She smiled and looped her arm through his.

"Sure, but someplace where no one can overhear the plans."

He winked. "Alone with Chicago's most sought-after bachelorette? Aren't I a lucky bastard?" He chuckled and she smirked as they headed toward the study.

Then the thought hit her. The guys always showed up whenever she was in town in Chicago for business or whatever. They ran different businesses in Chicago and Texas. Were they keeping an eye on her for Porter so closely that they would follow her here? Was this what their job offer was all about? Her temper flared as she thought about how stupid she was to be affected by their good looks and charms. They were being bodyguards as if she were some kid in need of a babysitter. Well hell. They would know soon enough just how independent and resourceful she really was. She knew more than they gave her credit for. Finding out who had been responsible for her abduction and why gave her the courage to take her life back. Oh yeah, Storm, Zin, Winter, Weston, and York would know soon enough how capable she was. Not even death intimidated her anymore.

Chapter 2

Storm Jones stood by the desk and shook his head.

"How the hell did she pull this off? Since when did she do business with the Russian fucking mob?" he said aloud to Zin as Zin pulled the information up on the computer screen.

Winter, Weston, and York stood there looking just as shocked as Storm felt.

"The woman is amazing, but this, this shit is going to cause some big-ass trouble. Andrei Renoke, that slimy Slavic bastard, is going to shit a brick," Winter said.

"How can we be sure that it was Aspen? I mean, she doesn't work for Dmitri. I know they spend a lot of time together and she's helped him with that organization he started, but still. I'm not sure she has the capabilities of pulling this off," York added.

"How could she? This is a twenty-million, maybe forty-million-dollar deal from what my sources say. Everyone is trying to figure out how Dmitri came out on top with the bidding on this construction job. Clearly Andrei used his political and mob ties to get Clarence to give his company a shot," Winter said.

Storm ran his hand through his hair.

"Hell, we know she's good at a lot of things besides retraining employees. It had to be her. We saw her with Gary Sparks at John Brothers's party. Read this description again of the unidentified woman who flew on Clarence's jet yet wasn't seen clearly by anyone to identify her," Storm told Zin.

"Okay, here is the description. The identity of the individual who apparently coordinated this multimillion-dollar deal with Cartwright

Productions stationed in Houston, Texas, is assumed to be a woman. Black hair, shapely figure, fashionable attire, and wearing a scarf tied around her hair and large sunglasses was clearly an attempt to hide her own identity from reporters. The unidentified woman, whose name was not on the flight list, disappeared in the private aircraft of Clarence Cartwright. No further information is available at this time," Zin read from the article.

"Aspen. You're right, Storm. It has to be her. I bet that plane went to the Caribbean where she was supposed to meet her friends and do that cruise thing. At least that's where Porter said she was," Weston added.

"Well, her brother would know. So if she was there, then maybe we're all mistaken," Weston added his point.

"I spoke to Porter that day, and he said that his sister had to fly somewhere for a meeting with some big shot and then would head back out to meet her friends. It was her. I'm telling you, we need to hire her to retrain our employees in Texas and get her out of Chicago. The security firm could have gotten a bad rap when that woman, Cherise, was abducted and held hostage by her ex. If our employees were better trained, they would have asked the right questions and identified the guy as a possible threat to the women not a long-lost brother. These people need better training," York told them.

"Either that or we're going to have to downsize this operation, focus on more of our non-legit commitments that bring in a shitload more money, and start doing these missing person investigations on our own. I don't know about you guys, but sitting in the back of a van for days at a time sucks," Weston said. They chuckled and agreed.

"I think we need to think about this more before we ask for Aspen's help. Our priority, and Porter's, is to keep Aspen out of Chicago and business like this. He is going to fucking flip out and he's not the only one. You guys do realize that Dmitri is going to hire our company and Brock, Smith, Rex, and Reno's company to do all the security work this project entails," Storm said.

"Holy shit. She just landed us the biggest contract of our business careers," Zin said aloud.

"She couldn't know about our illegal dealings could she? Like know we have been trying to get out and go legit? I mean is this an opportunity to do just that?" Weston said.

"She couldn't know. I mean she could hear rumors, maybe even believe some of them. But to go to this extent, and to wind up fucking over Andrei Renoke? Goddamn, I wonder why Dmitri didn't even talk her out of this," York added.

"Dmitri doesn't know how we feel about her, just that we're protective of her because of Porter. This job doesn't help us to get out of the business, it brings us deeper. We're under Dmitri Sanclare's payroll. You all know whom Dmitri answers to," Storm said.

"Whether Aspen was the one to negotiate this deal or not, Storm, if Dmitri got it, then we would have been hired for it. You'll do whatever you can to put a deeper wedge between you and her. It's not going to work," Zin stated.

They got quiet and Storm knew why. He started walking away from the computer.

"I know you don't want to go over this again, but we haven't seen Aspen in weeks. Not even by chance at the café downtown or at any events. I kind of miss seeing her," York admitted.

"Who the fuck doesn't, York? She's all we ever think about, but you know the deal, so why torture ourselves?" Zin said.

"We don't need to torture ourselves. It was torture enough knowing what she went through and not being able to find her sooner," Weston added.

"We've been over this. We watched over her with Porter and his team for the past six years with her only knowing about us the past three. It's better this way. She deserves better than a bunch of fucking retired Navy SEALs who have connections to the mob and could get her fucking killed," Storm stated firmly.

"Like fucking around in Andrei Renoke's business dealings isn't going to get her killed, or at minimum threatened or hurt by the fucker?" Winter asked.

"He's fucking right. The fuck already has his eyes on her and she doesn't even know it. She ignores just about every man that flirts with her. She won't see him for the dangerous man he is. If she finds out that Andrei was connected to that sex slave operation the Feds nearly busted, she might do something rash," York said.

They were all quiet and Storm thought about that a moment and something clicked.

"Like maybe sabotage a major multimillion-dollar business deal to get revenge on him for what she went through years ago?"

Winter whistled. "The shy, scared little seventeen-year-old who can't sleep in the dark sure has grown a set. That's if what you just said pans out to be true," Winter told Storm.

Storm looked at his team, his best friends and family.

"For her sake, I hope I'm wrong. The Russian mobs are not the type of individuals to screw over."

* * * *

Aspen Brooks took a sip of Bordeaux from the heavy crystal wine glass. The venue for the fundraising event was top notch as usual. This year Dmitri hosted it at the Fairmont, in Chicago. Through the elaborate dining area and along the massive windows a view of Grant and Millennium Park could be seen. It was impressive.

She scanned the area, trying her hardest to avoid particular people she had no tolerance for exchanging false pleasantries with. She wondered where India was. That woman couldn't stand still for too long. She more than likely was searching for tonight's lover. Her closest friend and fellow cohort when a Friday night of blowing off some steam and stress were needed, was currently flirting with a Brazilian gangster named Pantaro.

Aspen shook her head. Sometimes she wondered if India did this type of stuff to get under her brother Silas's skin. Even Aspen knew better than to mess with a Navy SEAL. Her own brother, Porter, was part of the same team as Silas, along with Piers, Ren, and Reid. Three very attractive men with bodies that could blow the socks off most male models. But Aspen wouldn't even think about hooking up with any of them.

No, it seemed she had more dangerous, exotic tastes when it came to men. She preferred the fantasy over the reality. She didn't do relationships, commitment, and closeness. In fact, she wondered if she were even normal. As most women, India included, talked about their sex lives—their fantasies fulfilled and guys they would do again, or even consider settling down with—Aspen was different. Her heart was sort of cold, distant, and surrounded by a protective shield. So much so that sex did nothing for her. She tried it three times and none were anything to reminisce about. She knew where that wall, that desperate need to keep on guard came from. She wasn't going to think about it now. All it would do was make for another sleepless night. It was bad enough that she was twenty-seven years old and couldn't sleep in the dark.

She heard the roar of laughter and then India's gasp. The woman sure did know how to lay on the charm. Five men gathered around her as she told some sort of story that had them intrigued and mesmerized by her beauty and her voice. It didn't hurt that she was a platinum blonde with big boobs and gorgeous blue eyes.

Aspen smiled and took another sip from her glass as she looked around the room again.

Dmitri Sanclare sure knew how to raise funds for his newest interest, the Star Haven. What had started out as a fundraising event to help underprivileged teens looking for ways to advance in high school and receive academic funding for college had turned into so much more. Now young students who spent time volunteering to tutor and assist younger members of the program earned free tuition for some of the top colleges in the nation. Eventually it led to career placements in Fortune 500 companies, too.

She worked for a few of those Fortune 500 companies. She attended as a representative along with the CEO, Brad Smothers, and CFO, Roger Benning. Of course they were schmoozing Dmitri Sanclare right now and trying to get him to partake in one of their new business ventures. Gary Sparks, their boss and a man known to be involved with the Slavs, wanted Dmitri's support. Word was that even Storm and his team were interested in taking over Sparks Industries.

Good luck with that.

Apparently the company was prime location with major international connections of the illegal and legal kind. But Dmitri was already flying high on the latest contract he'd landed, thanks to her. A silent partner, Aspen had just secured the deal of her life and all unbeknownst to anyone but Dmitri and the wealthy businessman and philanthropist, Clarence Cartwright.

In fact, she may have just helped Storm, Weston, York, Winter, and Zin get a few steps closer to taking over Sparks Industries.

She avoided Brad and Roger as they tried to get her attention. She knew those expressions. They were sinking and needed her help to persuade Dmitri. She wasn't going over there. Dmitri had a way about him that put Aspen on guard despite his sworn promise that he wouldn't try to seduce her. She wasn't sure what it was that put her on guard but she had learned at a very young age to trust her gut instincts. The man was a gangster. He also had a reputation of being a ladies' man, like most multimillionaires in business. She wouldn't be another notch in his Louis Vuitton belt just to help the men she worked for now and then land the deal.

Aspen was getting tired of the long hours and wild nightlife trying to keep up with all the networking in Chicago. She preferred Texas and even the smaller suburban towns like Tranquility and Salvation. She missed hanging out with her friends Gia and Mariana and hanging out at Casper's. It was so down to earth and nothing mattered but having fun, talking the days and nights away. No one cared that she had been a victim of violence or that she was wealthy. She could be herself. Let her hair down and get dirty working on one of the ranches, or even help Mariana at the art gallery in the city. It wasn't stressful. Besides the fact that Salvation, specifically Casper's, was filled with so many retired military that it gave her peace of mind and made her relax a little.

She was even getting tired of her job. It was becoming monotonous. The past year she had worked on slowly pulling away from the larger contracts and focusing on smaller businesses. Eventually she could take on jobs less frequently, but she was too young to retire. A life of beaching it on the shores of exotic resorts for the filthy rich didn't entice her. That hadn't been the incentive for all the strategic moves and business dealings she did.

All her hard work. The determination to establish a name for herself and be successful, a workaholic, was to maintain her sanity and ignore her fears. She worked herself to exhaustion in hopes that at night when her head hit the pillow she would be too tired to remember and to experience her terrible nightmares. No such luck.

So much had changed in the last year. Finding out who the real players were in a world of organized crime, sex slave businesses, and other illegal activities that nearly cost her life had become her obsession. She sought revenge, payback, a way of finding closure. All her strategic moves would either bring her closure she so desperately needed or would bring her death. She really didn't care. She had lost the ability to feel, to be capable of having love and being loved years ago as a teen. When others turned to addictions like alcohol, drugs, or even sex, she turned toward the adrenaline rush of negotiating and securing secret multimillion dollar deals. Now that she'd secured the silent partnership with Dmitri for the huge job and the bonus she received for securing it, she was set for life. She didn't have to work another day if she didn't want to. But what would she do? She wasn't the kind to sit around and do nothing. She didn't have a boyfriend or lover. Call her crazy, but she liked fixing messes. She enjoyed coming into a company, a business center, and retraining them to better serve the business and the owners' wallets. That was what got her the big bucks. That was what changed her life from having nothing to gaining opportunity.

She was street smart, business savvy, and a lot of men found that intimidating. She found it to be empowering. And thinking about settling down in a place like Salvation made her sad. Seeing all the couples, the ménage relationships in full bloom was depressing. It made her want things she could never have, nor could ever handle physically and emotionally. No, it seemed working herself to death was her destiny.

"Now this night just became completely tolerable. How are you, Aspen?"

She heard the deep voice and turned to see Demyan Sakoyvitcz. He was a Russian businessman who had ties to the Russian mob, an organization she was more than familiar with considering the silent owner of the company she worked for was his boss, a made man.

She showed the required respect for such an important man by lowering her head and greeting him. When she looked up, he was checking out her breasts before he focused on her eyes.

He took her hand and brought it to his lips, kissing the top of her skin.

"You look as beautiful as always, Aspen," he said in that thick Russian accent that had an instant effect on her body. She was only human. She liked a good, thick accent. Anything from Southern to Canadian and she was all intrigued and aroused.

"Thank you, Mr. Sakoyvitcz," she replied and his eyes squinted at her.

"Tsk, tsk. How many times do I have to tell you to please call me Demyan? We've known one another for a while now, Aspen. I think we can be more personal. In fact, I think you need to let me get you another drink."

He snapped his fingers and to the right she saw one of his security guy's stop a waiter carrying a tray of crystal glasses, and another one with a bottle of Bordeaux. In a flash the waiter was opening the bottle as the other one held two glasses that shook in his hand. Demyan had a way of intimidating people. Knowing the people she did, Aspen heard about Demyan's stint in prison for murder as well as a few other short terms behind bars for getting busted for illegal business infractions. The Feds were regulars to his home, or at least used to be before her boss's company, Sparks Industries, helped him clean up his paperwork.

"I prefer to keep things more businesslike, Demyan. I may be called to work for one of your companies again and would hate to overstep my boundaries."

"Aspen, you could never overstep your boundaries." He stared at her over the glass as he took a sip. His eyes, dark brown and filled with lies, held her gaze. She knew how to handle men like Demyan. She had been dealing with them most of her life, especially when Porter was serving and not around to protect her.

She swallowed hard. She didn't want to think about that. Why this man made her think such bad memories, she didn't want to analyze. It wasn't like every Russian mobster had something to do with illegal sex slave businesses. Nor did she have to find them all guilty by association. But it was habit. As far as she was concerned, most men involved with the Russian Mafia and bosses like Demyan, Iakov, and of course Andrei, were the enemy. Her enemy. Having only recalled bits and pieces of her near death, she learned that no one could be trusted. At least no one but her brother Porter, as far as she was concerned.

Under this red Vera Wang evening dress she'd paid a discounted price for was a capable, well-trained woman. Although she hoped to never use her knowledge of shooting guns, using a bow and arrows, skinning a deer, surviving in all weather conditions, and knowing how to place a person in a choke hold and killing them, it gave her an edge against men like Demyan. Intimidating, powerful, untrustworthy, and looking for a piece of ass, she would be the one to decide to proceed or disengage. Control was what kept her levelheaded and in charge.

"So what do you think about the event? You seem unimpressed." He pushed to converse.

"Oh, I wouldn't say that. It's elaborate and classy as usual. I wouldn't expect anything less from Dmitri." She looked around her, noticing the stares and looks she was receiving being caught conversing with Demyan Sakoyvictz.

"You know him well. You worked for him for a while didn't you?" he asked her and she cringed only slightly. There had been a rumor that she was sleeping with Dmitri around the same time there seemed to be some sort of bet as to who could land her as a lover. She immediately put a halt to it all by parading herself around town at all the major hot spots with Jester, a good friend from New York who stayed to visit for a month while he searched for employment opportunities. No one needed to know he preferred the company of men in his bed, not women. He'd enjoyed the little role playing so she didn't have to beg him to partake. She had the connections of getting him into all the major nightclubs, mostly owned by Russian mobsters and of course Storm Jones and his team of retired Navy SEALs who were so desperately trying to go legit. That wasn't happening. Thoughts of them made her belly tingle. They were gorgeous men.

"Now, Demyan, you know that was a rumor. I don't date or sleep with men I work for or have ever worked for."

"That's a terrible rule. One I'm hoping to break, tonight," he said as he reached out and caressed his knuckles down her cheek. He was quite charismatic, but still, he was cold, distant, a man capable of too many bad things. Plus, she didn't trust him at all. He, too, was interested in expanding Andrei's territory. That meant he was interested in her business associate's company, Sparks Industries. Gary Sparks would be smart to sell to Storm and Pro-Tech Industries.

"That's sweet of you to try, but I'm not biting," she replied with confidence.

He stepped a little closer, his eyes darker somehow, and his tone more disconcerting.

"It may not be up to you. *Ya khochu tebya*," he whispered next to her cheek. She tightened up immediately as he told her that he wanted her in Russian.

She tilted her head up toward him as he held her gaze. Then she nearly jumped when she felt the large hands on her shoulders from behind and Demyan's face take on an expression of anger for being interrupted.

"There you are. I thought I wouldn't have the opportunity to see you."

She turned around to see Storm Jones and couldn't help but to feel relieved from being saved from that uncomfortable situation.

She smiled as Storm leaned down and kissed her cheek, letting his lips linger against her skin. She wouldn't read into that. He was playing his role. Her protector. Her big brother. *Kill me now. He smells incredible, and his hands feel so good on me. I feel safe. That's nuts.*

"You look lovely as always, Aspen," he said, his eyes holding hers instead of immediately roaming over her breasts. She wasn't sure if she should be thrilled or annoyed. Storm was sexy, hard core, and big. Standing at nearly six foot four, he wore intimidation and that designer black tux too well. He made her thighs quiver and her pussy react, which was an impossible task to accomplish without physically touching those places. But Storm, Winter, Weston, York, and Zin seemed to have the capabilities of doing just that with only a glance or a bump.

"Storm, it's so nice to see you here. You know Demyan, I presume." She introduced the two men but knew that they knew one another. In fact, she thought there was some friction between them. More than likely over the fact that both men were interested in Sparks Industries. Both men had reputations.

They shook hands but Demyan had daggers in his eyes as Storm's hand remained on Aspen's shoulder then brushed down her arm to her waist where he held her by his side.

"It's nice to see you, Demyan. If you don't mind, I have some business to discuss with Aspen. Perhaps you could excuse us," he said in a tone that was obvious Storm didn't intend to let Demyan near her again. Demyan eyed Aspen over.

"I'll meet up with you later, Aspen. We'll set a date and time for dinner this week. Just the two of us." He took her hand and kissed it again, but his eyes roamed up to Storm, who for some reason appeared utterly pissed off.

Aspen wasn't going to read into Storm's expression. She knew he disliked the man for reasons that were none of her business. Whatever was between them, got her out of a potentially sticky situation. Demyan was the kind of man to not take her decline of his sexual advances too lightly.

* * * *

Storm was trying his hardest to control his temper. To see Aspen here, dressed so sexy and looking as gorgeous as usual, was difficult to ignore. From a distance she lit up the room and drew attention immediately with her sexy body and jet-black hair. Her gorgeous sage-green eyes were stunning as usual, enhanced with the eyeliner and mascara that made her thick, long lashes stand out even more.

He turned her around and led her further away from Demyan, a man who was after Aspen as more than his latest conquest.

"Thought you could use a little help getting away from him," he whispered as he guided her toward the food table. He knew that Zin was around, too. Zin had been pissed off to see Demyan hit on Aspen.

"You mean Demyan? He's harmless. I was fine, Storm," she said, glancing up at him. She was so petite compared to him even though she was average height, about five foot five. Standing this close to her, he took advantage of the feel of her hip, the curve of her ass, and the scent of her shampoo. He could imagine himself lying beside her in bed after hours of making love and getting lost inside of her. But the reality was that he could never have her. Nor could his men. Their jobs and their connection to illegal activities and being at high risk for attempted conflict weren't the right environment for Aspen. She had gone through enough years ago.

His chest tightened at the memory. She nearly died.

"I think you underestimate Demyan's abilities, Aspen. The man doesn't take no for an answer."

"I seemed to be handling him fine, Storm," she snapped at him.

He paused near the banquet table, holding her upper arm as he stared down into her face. He could see the defiance, the stubbornness and assertiveness that was all Aspen. She was tough. But not tough enough.

"I thought otherwise. You need to be more careful. Men like Demyan are not good for you. What ever happened to that guy Jester from New York?" He saw her eyes widen in shock and then quickly recover and appear pissed off. What had he said to anger her so?

She pulled her arm from his hold.

"Listen, Storm, I appreciate the brotherly protectiveness, but I don't need it. Why don't you run along and go pick tonight's special for you and your *team* to share." She abruptly turned around and walked away toward the ladies' room.

He was stunned. Totally caught off guard. How the hell did he just piss her off like that? What did she mean by pick tonight's special for him and his team? Did she mean a bed mate? She knew they shared. Hell, half the men in the place had a lover they shared or were searching for one for tonight. He watched as men took in the sight of Aspen as she sashayed toward the ladies' room.

None of these men were taking Aspen home with them. Not if he and his team had a say in it.

"What the hell happened?" He turned to see Zin with an expression of humor on his face.

"I think I pissed her off."

Zin chuckled then took a sip from his glass of red wine.

"It looked that way. You're usually real smooth with the ladies. How did it go wrong?"

"I steered her away from that dick Demyan. That's all that matters."

"Sure it is. She looked good. It's been two months since we've seen her. Did you ask about her trip?" Zin asked.

Storm shook his head, but he knew where she had been. A two-week cruise on a private yacht with five of her friends, then a stint in the Caribbean with business, and she'd returned two days ago in time to be here for Dmitri. That was another guy who had an interest in Aspen. Perhaps more business than pleasure, but still, Dmitri did have the reputation of fucking most of his female staff. He hoped that Aspen wasn't sleeping with Dmitri. He'd known the man for many years. Had some deep ties to him, too. Dmitri knew where Storm stood with Aspen. He'd be beyond pissed off if Dmitri were after her.

With long, jet-black hair, incredible sage-green eyes that stood out so bright against her olive complexion, and a body made for sin, she had a trail of men behind her wanting that body. But she was more than just a sexy, attractive woman for a man to show off by his side. She was intelligent, funny, friendly, and had a way about her that was modest, not stuck up. She was tough, too. That was why so many men hit on her and tried to get her attention. Why she declined except for that guy Jester, who she dated for a while and even lived with, he didn't know.

Storm felt his anger grow stronger. That had been the worst four months of their lives. Knowing she was seeing someone and that he shared her bed really fucking aggravated him. Zin, Weston, York, and

Winter were hell to live with, and he wasn't any better. They were glad to see her dump the guy. But she was too perfect to not have another boyfriend soon. It was inevitable.

There was nothing he could do about it. He and his team led dangerous lives despite their efforts to go more legit. With Sotoro trying to fuck them along with unidentified others, he needed to remain focused on the businesses throughout the US they had. They could use Aspen's professional help in reorganizing their team of employees here in Chicago as well as in Texas. Despite his promise to himself and his team to stay clear of the woman they longed for, she could be an asset to their business. But she also had inside information on their business enemies. Information she may not be willing to give up because of her loyalty to confidentiality. He couldn't fault her for that either. She would always be special to him and the team. But the fact that she was Porter's sister, and simply being unable to give her the life she deserved, he needed to keep his dick out of this.

Aspen deserved a legit man. She also didn't seem interested in sharing herself with more than one man at once. At least he didn't want to think of her being made love to by any man or men except for him and his team. They all wanted her. Hell, they talked about making a move, but the consequences seemed to outweigh their own happiness. If Aspen got involved with them, she would be in more danger than ever before. In fact, their enemies could try to kill her. No, they couldn't do that to her. She needed a good life, a perfect life made for a woman as sweet and capable as her. He tried to keep his distance from her and not show his true feelings. He warned his team to hide them as well or it could put her life in danger. But every time he thought about her, he thought about who she was sleeping with, who got to hold her in his arms and inhale that delicious scent of her perfume. That just fucked with his head and increased the possessive feeling he'd had since day one.

He thought about her more often than he wanted to admit. He didn't need to ask the others if they thought about her, too. Zin and York would be pleased if Aspen accepted a position working for them. But she didn't seem ready to leave her current position where she was. At least he didn't think she would want to. She was making crazy money. Sparks Industries seemed to keep her on permanently although she said her work was contractual. Hell, if things went well between Storm, his team, and Gary Sparks, Aspen might just wind up being an employee of theirs after all. Wouldn't that be nice?

He imagined what he would do to her, if there weren't all these restrictions and fears for her life. She would be his whenever he wanted her. In the office, over his desk, in the private elevator, or even in their penthouse where he and his team could share her.

That was a fantasy. None of them would be so selfish as to bring death to her doorstep and destroy her chance at happiness. No, they had to deny the feelings they had for her and pretend to be the good brothers watching out for their best friend's sister.

He sought her out and once again saw her talking, socializing with three businessmen he knew pretty well. They were good men. Each would make a great husband for Aspen.

He felt his gut wrench in anger and disgust. Who the fuck was he kidding? He didn't ever want to see her with another man in a romantic relationship ever.

She lived in a penthouse suite in one of the best buildings in the city owned by him and his team, and had an outstanding reputation in the business world as well as amongst their own family and friends.

No, staying clear, perhaps protecting her from afar was best.

"You look about ready to kill someone," Zin told Storm.

"I'm fine. Let's see if we can get a few minutes of Dmitri's time. We have that business to discuss and finalize."

"Well, then you better gain control of that jealous anger from seeing Aspen with Demyan. She's currently walking arm and arm with Dmitri right now," Zin said.

Storm looked across the room and exhaled with his fists by his side. Sure as shit, there was Dmitri, the fucking bastard, with his hand practically on Aspen's ass. As she laughed at something one of his guards said to her, she turned and lost her smile immediately.

There stood Andrei Renoke.

* * * *

"Dmitri, why do you insist on asking me out? You know my answer already. We've been friends far too long and I know your history with women."

"Oh come on now, Aspen, you and I would make a fabulous couple. My good looks, your natural beauty and charm, never mind business sense. Have I thanked you enough for the Clarence job you grabbed right out from underneath Andrei's fingertips?"

She chuckled, knowing it was more for personal satisfaction that she pulled the multimillion-dollar construction job right from under Andrei's nose. The slimy bastard deserved to die for what he had done and continued to get away with. Just as she laughed, she locked gazes with the scumbag himself. Anger boiled through her bloodstream and she wished so badly they weren't here at a fundraising event. Perhaps a shooting range with his head as the target would make her happier.

"Once again, Dmitri, you've outdone yourself. This is quite the affair," he said, giving Dmitri the once-over but her, he let his eyes intentionally take their time looking her body over. It gave her the creeps as Aspen unconsciously stepped back. But Andrei reached for her hand and brought it to his lips as he pulled her toward him. His forcefulness and show of authority seemed to not only get under her skin but Dmitri's as well.

Dmitri placed his hand on her shoulder, causing her to stand between the two men, too close for comfort. She tried pulling her hand from Andrei's but he didn't allow it. She felt the gun and holster as he pulled her snug against him. The man had audacity. But as much as she despised him, she, too, had to play her role and show respect.

"Mr. Renoke. It's nice to see you." She lowered her head and eyes.

He inhaled against her hair and she tilted her head up, shocked by his move. They locked gazes and she felt the shiver of fear roll up her spine. She was playing with fire. Had been since she took on the job Dmitri offered her in sealing the business deal. She didn't want to be this close to the man. He had an aura of power, death, and darkness that told every nerve ending in her body to retreat and just let him talk and play his role. She looked toward Dmitri.

"Dmitri, you didn't tell me that you were having such big shots attending the gathering tonight."

She felt Andrei's hand slide down her arm to her waist. He gave her hip a squeeze as he softly chuckled. "I'm surprised he failed to mention he invited me weeks ago. I usually don't have the time to attend these events. However, I heard that you would be here, Ms. Brooks."

He pulled her against his side as if he now had possession of her.

Oh shit.

"You're very smooth, Mr. Renoke. Do lines like that always work with the ladies?"

He squinted at her and looked her body over then back toward Dmitri, who still kept a hand on her shoulder. She wondered if there would be a tug of war over her. She hoped to not make a scene. It seemed they were already drawing some attention.

"I would like a moment alone with Aspen, Dmitri. I'm sure you don't mind."

"Oh, well, we were discussing something important. Perhaps later would work better?" Dmitri asked, but Andrei shook his head and a moment later she noticed two of his guards standing near the side, looking ready to cause a scene. She wouldn't want that on her conscience.

"It's okay, Dmitri. I'm fine and whatever Andrei Renoke has to say to me must be important," she challenged, and Andrei chuckled low.

"Shall we?" Andrei stuck out his arm for her to loop hers through and to walk with him.

She wasn't stupid. She knew not to piss off the Russian mobster. Well, at least to his face. Behind closed doors, during a huge business deal? That was a different story. The only way to seek revenge against a man like Andrei was to hit him in the wallet. She could snap a little here and there, and let him know he didn't have control over her, but she also knew his resources. If he were truly bent about the business opportunity she took out from under him, then he would make her aware of the consequences soon enough. They walked along the crowd of people and out toward the balcony. It was a bit too secluded, almost intimate for her liking, but she had no choice. She would hear the man out.

He turned around to face her as two of his guards took position at the entrance to the balcony. Her heart pounded inside of her chest, but she had been around mobsters long enough to know not to show intimidation. Especially around this man she disliked immensely.

He eyed her over from head to toe and pulled his bottom lip between his teeth as he watched her. He was older, by at least ten years, but not quite fifty. With dark black hair he definitely dyed, and a well-maintained body, the man was filthy rich and well feared in certain circles.

"So what was it that you wanted to discuss?" she asked him, trying not to show any fear even though that was foolish of her.

He stepped closer and she found her back against the railing that looked out over the city. His hand fell to her waist and the other over her shoulder and against the stone balcony railing.

She could smell his cologne combined with expensive cigars as the sleeve of his tux brushed against her bare shoulder.

"Your business savvy may cost you a bit of making up with me," he said, eyeing over her lips as if he were going to kiss her. She tilted her head up with confidence despite his six-inch difference in height and his position in front of her. He squeezed her hip and let his hand glide along her ribs.

"Making up for what?"

"Well let's see, Aspen. How about sneaking behind my back and stealing a forty-million-dollar construction job right out from under my nose and giving it to that weasel Dmitri? Do you realize how many people you've pissed off?"

"I don't know what you're talking about, Andrei."

His grip tightened. "Are you really going to play this game with me? I know it was you. I know you were on his yacht, had meetings with Clarence. Maybe even fucked him on his yacht to seal the deal." He brushed his thumb along the underside of her breast.

She inhaled. "I don't spread my legs to seal deals. Never have, and never will. I would check your sources. Sir," she added with attitude.

He gave a short chuckle and looked over her breasts. "Yes, I've heard you're very particular with who you spread your legs for. But you see, Aspen, you've gone and got involved in something that you should never have touched. I've allowed you to get this far in business."

"Allowed me?"

"You negotiated a deal that was set to be mine."

"The construction job was Dmitri's opportunity eight months ago. He called me and hired me on as a consultant with experience in all aspects of this type of business because he was too busy with a few other business ventures he was partaking in."

He pressed closer, his hand inches below her breast.

She gasped and he used his other hand to grip the back of her neck under her hairline. Teeth clenched, he whispered to her, "It was mine and you fucked me over. Do you know what I do to women like you who think they can play in a man's world?"

She knew she was in trouble, but then again she knew when she negotiated with Clarence in Texas for the huge job that she was indeed manipulating the situation to take Andrei and his company out of the running for the job. After all, because of his participation in an illegal sex slave business, she had been abducted, tortured, and nearly raped before she was sold to the highest bidder in some corrupt underground operation. She didn't even remember being saved she was so drugged out from the sedatives they forced on her during transport. The man was a monster.

She needed to play this cool. To make him think she would respect him because of his position and his role as a mob boss. Truth was, she hoped he got killed in one of those old-fashioned hits. The kind where some hit man filled Andrei with lead as he fired off a semiautomatic machine gun, tearing his flesh to pieces. The thought sickened her.

"You don't scare me, Andrei. I didn't do anything wrong. I was negotiating a deal for a close friend. It was all business."

He raised one eyebrow at her. "I should scare you. I can make you disappear. For good this time," he threatened her.

Was he admitting to being involved in her abduction? Was she supposed to play dumb here? Maybe tell him to go to hell and fuck off? He had a gun on him. He could take her out right here. She could reach for the gun and blow his head off. That would take courage and her life would be over. Was he worth it? As these thoughts went through her head, she realized that she felt nothing. Not accomplished. Not proud. Not stronger. She didn't feel scared or fearful. No, she felt nothing. He made her this way.

"You're admitting to taking me from my family years ago and trying to sell me as some sex slave?" she asked, her voice cracking with anger.

He smirked as he looked her lips over again. "I'm not admitting to anything. I'm just saying, knowing through my close sources what happened to you, if it was me it wouldn't have happened that way. You would be all mine. The guys screwed up, probably sedated you and shipped you out. It was a major screwup. What fool would give up this body, this spunk, and these tits to another man? Not when he can keep you as his own sex slave to fuck whenever he wanted." He caressed the hair from her cheek and rubbed his thumb along the skin on her cheek.

She gave a snort and stared up at him, wanting nothing more than to punch the pompous bastard in the mouth. "You ruined me. Made me feel nothing for anything. So you're pissed off about a business deal you lost out on? That's your problem. I'm sure you can make it up somewhere along the way in your corrupt, violent world."

"It would be my pleasure to take you the right way this time, Aspen. But you see, there's so much more at stake here. More than you can even begin to comprehend."

"You have some nerve coming here and talking to me like this after all this time. I should have died."

"You didn't though. Next time I'll handle you myself."

Her eyes widened. "Next time?" she asked, feeling and sounding outraged. The sick fuck was out of his mind.

He ran his thumb along her throat and then gripped it snuggly, shocking her.

She reached up and covered his hand as he leaned closer, maintaining the choke hold. His mouth was right next to her lips. She could feel his spittle and his teeth graze her mouth.

"Don't fuck with me, Aspen. I will get you back. I will make it so that you'll never see your brother or any other asshole who thinks it's their job to protect you. You think Storm and his buddies can protect you from me? You're wrong. I'm more powerful than them. They're weak. They want out of a life they're connected by blood from. It doesn't work that way. You're going to get them and your brother killed. How is that for just business?" He applied pressure to her throat, shocking her and making her panic. Would he strangle her right here on the balcony where hundreds of people stood only ten feet from the entrance? She was shaking, her eyes wide with fear, and he smiled.

"One day I'll have you all alone and to myself. You'll learn the obedience necessary to be my woman. When I call upon you, you better come. If you don't, then the consequences will be great. Those men in your life that you think can protect you will die because of you. Do you understand?" he asked. He pressed his body snugger against hers and cupped her breast as he still held her by the throat with his other hand.

"I understand," she softly whispered then tried swallowing, but he held her tightly.

A moment later she heard a grunt. As Andrei and her looked, his men were pressed against the walls with guns at their throats, and both Zin and Storm were standing there along with Dmitri and his men. Storm and Zin stepped closer.

Andrei had already released his hold on her and she started coughing.

"Get the fuck away from her. I don't ever want to see you near her again," Storm threatened as two men stood by Andrei and began walking him out.

"There's no need for hysterics, Storm. Aspen and I were just discussing something important. I think we're clear on things now. Aren't we, Aspen?" Andrei asked as he held her gaze.

She nodded.

"Get him out of here. Escort him and his buddies to their car. Keep your hands off of Aspen," Dmitri ordered as three big men in suits took over removing Andrei. But one look at Andrei and Aspen knew this wasn't over.

She was in a shitload of trouble. As she turned around to face the balcony and catch her breath, her body was numb. No tears emerged.

She never cried. That was how separated she was from emotions, from feeling anything. Although she was physically shaken up from Andrei's threatening hold, she still had an ability to lock down her emotions and hold them inside.

Never show weakness and fear again.

* * * *

Zin hurried to Aspen's side as Storm argued with Dmitri over keeping an eye on Aspen and how he let Aspen be alone with that man. He felt his own blood boiling and he damned himself for listening to Storm about not making a scene the moment they caught sight of Andrei. The man had no boundaries, especially when it came to women and manhandling them. Why was he even speaking with Aspen? Why did she walk away with him to the balcony?

"Aspen?" he whispered.

"I'm fine, Zin. I just need a minute."

He stepped closer, placed his hand on her shoulder, and she tried stepping away. She was scared but she was stubborn and tough, always having something to prove.

"It's okay. You're okay now," he assured her. She turned to look at him and he saw the fear in her glistening sage eyes and his heart ached. Then he locked on to the redness on her throat.

"That fucking bastard." He reached for her and pulled her closer to examine the marks.

He gently glided his thumb along the skin that wasn't marked.

"What's wrong?" Storm asked and Aspen looked away.

"I'm fine. He was just trying to scare me."

"Well, he did a good job," Zin told her then reached for her chin and gripped it, making her look up into his eyes. She was so freaking beautiful. He wanted to pull her into his arms and hold her tight. Take that fearful expression from her face and make her see that she could lean on him, on the rest of the team. Yet here they were, having to hide their feelings from a woman they honestly already loved.

"We're leaving."

"No, Zin, I'm fine. The last thing I want to do is go home," she said.

"Why?" Storm asked in that aggressive, deep tone that was all commanding. Zin could see Aspen cringe from it.

"It's… There are more people here. It's better."

"With us is where you're safest. We need to find out what exactly went down here and why Andrei is interested in bothering you."

"He didn't bother me. He was just being typical Andrei. He thinks women are second-class citizens."

Zin gripped her arms and gave her a slight shake. "Goddamn it, Aspen, he had you by the fucking throat and pinned against the fucking balcony." Zin kept his teeth clenched and Aspen just stared up at him in shock. Her sage-green eyes sparkled and he couldn't resist. Her scent, the feel of being this close to her, knowing that some dick tried to hurt her and he needed to step in along with Storm sent any patience he had out the window. He was mad with possessiveness and need.

"Aspen," he whispered right before he lowered his mouth to hers and kissed her.

* * * *

Aspen didn't know what had come over Zin or her, but the moment Zin kissed her, nothing else seemed to matter. The man was every woman's fantasy come true.

He held her tight and explored her mouth with passion and need. She found herself giving in to his quest to take whatever he wanted from her. It was magical, different, overwhelming to say the least. She felt his hands move along her arms to her ass and pull her snugger against his chest. She gripped his back and rocked her body against him as they both moaned.

"Zin. Zin!"

The sound of Storm's commanding tone and his order penetrated their dazed state and Zin pulled slowly from her mouth.

She stared up at him and his dark blue eyes that stood out in contrast to his onyx hair.

"What the fuck are you thinking? She's Porter's sister. Get the fucking car. I'll get her downstairs to the garage," Storm ordered.

Aspen looked to Zin but his face showed no expression as he took his order and disappeared, leaving her standing there feeling like an easy target for any man tonight.

Storm stared at her, looked her over and then spoke into the cell phone she hadn't even realized he was holding.

"Affirmative. Get to the penthouse pronto. Zin will update you any moment."

He disconnected the call and grabbed her upper arm.

"Let's move. Smile so no one thinks anything is going on."

She was annoyed, and even angry at his tone, and his treatment of her. She was still trying to recover from Zin's kiss and the encounter with Andrei. She didn't need Storm's help or for him to go blabbing to her brother and his friends about what happened. As soon as they got into the elevator along with one of Storm's newly appointed guards, she pulled from his hold.

He glared at her and stepped into her space, causing her back to wedge up against the wall. Damn it, she hadn't expected the surge of attraction she felt to Storm. His big muscles, the way the tux hugged his gorgeous body, and his incredible good looks. The man was so breathtaking, even with that bit of scruff that always seemed to appear late in the evenings.

She knew more about Storm and his team members than she could ever let on. They had been somewhat of an obsession for her. Something she could never entertain, never show her attraction to but only admire from afar. She couldn't face the fact that Zin kissed her the way he did.

"I'm not messing around with you, Aspen. Andrei is not a man to underestimate."

She wanted to tell Storm that Andrei shouldn't underestimate her, but that was her anger talking. She knew this wasn't going to be the end of this situation with Andrei. He was pissed that she secured that construction deal for Dmitri when he felt that it was his. Andrei assumed he had Clarence convinced about the numbers, but he was being pompous and overcharging when there was already plenty of money to make. It also gave her a nice hefty bonus. But she was also securing the existence of Pro-Tech Industries so that Storm, Winter, Zin, York, and Weston wouldn't have it stolen out from underneath them.

Didn't they know that Sotoro was working with Andrei, Demyan, and Iakov? As much as she felt on edge with Dmitri, he had given her a lot of inside information on Storm and his crew. Did Storm think she was so stupid she wouldn't know he was a made man? It insulted her intelligence and what little connection if any they had. But now Andrei threatened their lives and Porter's. She would need to talk to her brother and get him to take the necessary precautions.

She turned away and Storm stared at her. She felt his gaze upon her and inhaled his cologne, his manliness. Everything about Storm was mysterious and dark. Men feared him. Hell, even Dmitri somewhat did. Andrei didn't, but being made a fool wasn't going to win any points. Andrei could harass Storm and Zin for interfering in his affair and getting him removed from the venue tonight.

"You shouldn't have gotten involved. You or Zin," she said without thinking.

"Are you out of your mind? He had you by the throat." He slammed his palm against the wall. His guard kept his face forward as she looked from him back to Storm.

"That's Andrei's MO. To him women are good for only a few things. The respect isn't there and he was pissed off."

The elevator doors opened and the guard who accompanied them looked out first and then headed to the awaiting car. Storm looked around and then guided Aspen toward the car. He had a tight hold on her hip and she wondered if he would manhandle her, he was so enraged. Her heels clicked and clacked on the concrete flooring as she tried to keep up with his long strides. She got inside and he slid along the seat next to her.

"Why was Andrei pissed off at you?" he asked her as the car began to roll through the parking garage and onto the busy city streets.

She kept her face straight ahead. She knew that Storm and his team would know by now that she was the one to secure the deal. What did she expect? A thank-you for landing them the job of their lives?

"Because I secured a new construction deal for Dmitri right out from under Andrei's nose. He wanted that deal, twenty million plus, maybe more by the time all is done. It was just business. Don't act like you don't know everything about it."

She kept a straight face and didn't turn to look at him. He was silent, and she felt uneasy about it. She didn't like feeling exposed by Storm. There was just something about him that affected her so. She knew his reputation and she knew to never lie to him. When Storm or Winter asked a question, the person better answer and be truthful or there would be hell to pay. She respected them.

"Revenge has its side effects, Aspen."

She swung her head to look at him. She hadn't expected that response. Like he had a clue as to why she wanted revenge and that revenge was indeed her motivation in screwing Andrei out of the job that should have been his. Nothing would ever be enough. No amount of money made would take away her nightmares or her experience as a seventeen-year-old woman who was beaten, nearly raped, and sold to be some foreign asshole's sex slave. Andrei owned and operated that business. There were others involved. Others she screwed over, ruining their businesses, their future, and making them suffer. But Storm, Zin, York, Weston, Winter, and her brother Porter didn't know what she was capable of or how she sought revenge on those unpunished. So Storm hadn't a clue either. He probably only knew about her abduction because of Porter and his need to keep her out of Chicago and away from Andrei.

"You're playing with fire, little girl. You don't know what men like Andrei are capable of."

She snorted in annoyance. He hadn't a fucking clue. She could tell him right now. She could tear into him and let the almighty Storm know exactly how she knew firsthand what a prick bastard Andrei really was. But that would mean showing a vulnerability she had given up a long time ago. A weakness that only flashbacks brought on that she shared with no one ever. Not even the fact that she could have sworn she recognized the voice of one of the men who took her from the facility where women were being held before being shipped out. When she heard that voice was when she would truly be tested.

Storm didn't know what she went through. At least not all of it. Maybe Porter told him about her so they could watch over her when Porter and his team weren't nearby? If that were the case, then that explained why they kept their distance. They didn't want her because of what happened to her and because they saw her as their sister. Well, except maybe Zin. He was the one to kiss her, but even that could have been pure lust.

"Your brother is going to find out about this."

She looked at him. "That's your job isn't it? Try to keep an eye on me. Keep me in Texas where it's safe from mobsters and cruel business dealings? I had that under control. I don't need babysitters. You can drop me off at my home and go back to the party or whatever. I've got this."

Storm slammed his hand down on the leather seat between them as he faced her.

"Are you delusional? Were you not present mentally during that confrontation? He had you by the throat. His hands were all over you, cupping your breasts, showing through actions that he wants you and can take whatever he wants. He was going to make you leave with him."

She shook her head. "No man can make me do anything I don't want to do, Storm. It's over. Drop me off at my place."

"It's not over. You've got yourself a situation, baby girl, and you're going to need some help." She shot a look at him and was annoyed at the way he called her baby girl. She wasn't some kid. He always saw her as the teenage girl who was Porter's baby sister. They all did. Except maybe for Zin, who actually had the balls to act on his apparent attraction to her. Kudos to Zin. So why was she feeling disappointed that Storm wasn't pulling her across the leather seat and onto his lap so he could kiss her the way Zin had? Because he didn't have the same feelings for her that she had for him. For all of them.

Maybe she did have a death wish. Maybe she really needed to walk away and get out of the city completely? Away from Andrei, away from the painful memories of Chicago and the constant cutthroat business politics she needed to handle on a regular basis. Perhaps it was time for a change.

* * * *

"Now what? You think he's going to just drop this?" York Reiss asked Aspen as he sat in the chair across from her. It wasn't so difficult to be angry right now. Seeing her in the sexy evening gown, hair all done up, makeup, cleavage exposed like a goddess and his temper flared. York longed to touch her, taste her, hell, just hold her in his arms and inhale her perfume. She filled his every dream and fantasy and yet he couldn't have her.

"This is not your problem. Any of yours. He'll get over it," she replied as she recrossed her legs, showing off a bit more thigh than the last time she shifted positions on the couch.

"You think so? You think Andrei will get over the fact that you pulled a multimillion-dollar deal right out from underneath his feet?" Weston asked her. She looked at him and then glared at Storm and Zin.

"Maybe not so easily now, since Storm and Zin decided to go all crazy on him and toss him out of the venue like some loser. He has a reputation to maintain. Besides, if he should be bent at anyone, it should be Dmitri. He's the one who made out in all of this. Listen, I have no regrets about this business deal. You guys are the ones blowing this out of proportion. It was just business, an opportunity that I couldn't pass up. Besides, your company made out from this deal big-time," she said and stood up.

York stood up, too, and blocked her from walking away. He held her gaze, looking down into her sage-green eyes. He towered over her. They all did. He wanted to protect her and possess her and it was getting ridiculous to fight the attraction he felt. Before he could say a word, Storm spoke.

"Sit your ass down. This is not over."

"I don't take orders from you, Storm. I'm not part of your team," she scolded.

York wanted to say she already was, but that would be a lie, a fantasy never to become reality. They tried to go legit with the business. It just wasn't feasible without coming off as weak and losing just about everything. Aspen would need a man, men, to take good care of her in every aspect.

"Do you know what it means to have a mob boss on your ass? Do you have any fucking clue what revenge he'll seek knowing you ripped him off from that kind of huge payoff? No! Apparently fucking not. How damn stupid are you?" Storm yelled and York was shocked. He was being pretty hard on her.

Aspen stepped forward and looked about ready to press her finger into Storm's chest then thought better of touching him.

"What? What do you think you're capable of doing?" Storm challenged her.

She shoved at his chest and he stepped toward her, looking down at her.

"Go to hell. I did what I had to."

She went to turn away and Storm grabbed her wrist and pulled her against him.

"He wants you. Will take everything, even this body from you against your will."

"He'll have to kill me first."

"You don't think he won't?"

"I don't care either way."

"What?" Winter said from behind Storm.

She looked away. She was angry, wanted revenge, and York could understand that.

Storm reached forward and cupped her cheek. He gripped her chin to force her to look up into his eyes. "I don't believe you."

"That I could care less about living or dying?" She snorted softly under her breath. "Why do you care?

Storm's eyes darkened, his grip tightened, and he covered her mouth and kissed her.

In a flash Winter was behind her supporting her back, running his hands along her shoulders and arms as Storm devoured her moans and stroked his tongue in exploration in her mouth. She gripped his tux. His hands dug into her hair, her scalp, and both men pressed their bodies against hers when suddenly he pulled back gasping for breath. She nearly lost her balance but Winter was there to steady her.

"You aren't resistant to any male who wants to take from you what he wants. He won't accept no. You're too weak to handle men as powerful as Andrei."

Her anger rose and York was shocked, too. Storm had just made her feel used. He was showing her how weak she was under a man's control.

"You're such an asshole."

"I'm proving a point. You're not meant for this type of life. Dealing with mobsters, being threatened and used for your body. He'll make you spread your legs and he'll take your soul."

She took a deep breath and then released it.

"I'm not going round and round with you over this. What's done is done. Now please leave. I'm tired, I have an early meeting in the morning and I need my mind fresh, not boggled down with your hysterics and your mind games. I appreciate the escort home and the assistance with Andrei, but it ends here. I don't need your protection. I don't need you playing games with my head, taking what you want from me to show me how weak I am and how easily a man can use me and trick me. I've been dealing with men like you for years. I can handle this myself. I'm glad we're clear that I mean nothing to you either. Get out."

"Aspen, please listen to us." York tried to calm the situation but one look into Aspen's eyes and he knew that Storm had truly hurt her.

They watched her walk away and go into her bedroom way across the room in the upscale penthouse.

"That's what she thinks," Winter said under his breath.

"Let's go. We're done here," Storm said and turned to leave.

"Are we leaving her unattended?" York asked, fully concerned for her well-being.

"She doesn't want our help, York," Storm snapped at him as they all headed out of her penthouse.

York was fuming. As much as Storm tried to deny his feelings for Aspen, it was obvious that he cared about her. He was suffering as much as the rest of them were. They all had enemies similar and even worse than Andrei. They would think nothing of hurting Aspen, taking her, torturing her, or even killing her to get back at any of them. What kind of life would that be for Aspen?

But the fact that Storm was going to leave her place with her unguarded wasn't right. His persistence to pretend he didn't have feelings was getting in front of his better judgment. Aspen was still important to them and was Porter's sister.

"She needs protection," York said aloud in the elevator. They were squeezed into the small box. They were all too big, too tall for such small spaces.

"She made her decision," Storm snapped. York looked at the others. They kept their faces forward but he could see the change of emotion in their eyes. Aspen did that to them.

"I don't think you're right. I think she needs protection. Andrei could come here or send some of his guys to mess with her and scare her further."

"I'm the commander. I give the orders," Storm snapped.

The elevator doors opened.

"I don't get you. I know you care about her. We all fucking do. You couldn't resist kissing her, tasting her, and then you turn around and act like it was a fucking game and basically slap her across the face. She's in danger. We get that clearly. So we can't have her. We can't involve her in the life paths we chose or she could get hurt or even killed. I get it. But leaving her unguarded is just asking for something to happen to her. Why are you being such an asshole?" York raised his voice and walked ahead to the SUV. That was when he saw one of their well-trained security guys talking into his wrist mike.

York glanced back at Storm. Storm got into the SUV and Winter into the driver's side. The others joined and then York got in.

So his commander wasn't such an asshole after all. He had placed a team of security at Aspen's penthouse. She was going to be safe. They would protect her no matter what. But that kiss, the way Storm poured so much emotion into it and how receptive Aspen was to it just further clarified the mutual desire. If she was in danger anyway, then why couldn't they claim her as their woman? Wouldn't that in itself make Andrei Renoke have second thoughts about fucking with her and with them?

If they made that move, yes, Aspen would be protected under them as their woman, but she would also become an even greater target to more men like Andrei who wanted to take over their ties with the head of the Russian organization. They were fucked.

* * * *

Aspen heard the door slam and knew they'd all left. She walked out of her room and made sure to check the penthouse. She couldn't help but to be shocked at the disappointed feeling she had to find they had all left. Not even one of them were assigned to stay as a guard? More than likely it would be a stranger if Storm even gave the order for someone to stand around and watch over her. They couldn't be bothered with the task themselves. No, Storm proved how little she meant to him by kissing her like he did. By using his body, his lips, tongue, and mouth to bring out the inner desire she had locked away and tried unsuccessfully to hide from him and the team tonight. He was right. She was weak. Weak when it came to one of them kissing her, showing any sign even miniscule that they wanted her in a sexual way. God, he was a fantastic fucking kisser. Add in Winter standing behind her, his thick, hard body, the holster hidden on his waist wedged up against her back and fuck yeah she would have spread her thighs for them. For one night of pleasure. But Storm showed her how little she meant to them. How degrading he made her feel and like just another woman they could fuck if they wanted to. She hadn't even tried to resist, to play a hint of denial to his game. A fucking game? He played her. How could she have been so stupid?

She was smarter than this. No man broke down her defenses. None. Goddamn it, Storm and his team could. She could never let anything like that happen again. They proved she meant nothing to them but a commitment of protection because of Porter.

Damn, they would call Porter and he would freak out. He was out of the country on business so avoiding his calls would be her saving grace.

She looked around the room as she locked the bolt on the front door. How could they leave her after Andrei threatened her like he did tonight?

Why was she disappointed? She knew they didn't care for her. In fact Zin kept his distance. When she caught him watching her, he glared and turned away. His kiss meant nothing. It was probably a way to control her just like Storm used kissing her to prove his point.

She heard her cell phone ringing and reached for her purse. She pulled it out and saw the missed calls. As it rang she realized it was Dmitri. She answered the call as she headed back to her room.

"Are you okay?"

"I'm fine."

"They were pissed off. I wasn't expecting that show of aggression from Storm and Zin."

"Neither was I. But they do take watching over me for Porter and being my big brothers very seriously."

"You saved their company and you revealed the rat who is working with Andrei behind their backs."

"I did? I thought you said you weren't sure."

"Oh, I was almost positive Sotoro was in on this scam all along, but not Gary Sparks."

"What? Dmitri you can't be serious. Gary is getting ready to sell Sparks Industries and I've been talking up Storm and the team. You think he's been going behind Storm's back and working out a deal with Andrei?"

"It seems that way. If Andrei gets that company, he'll go after Pro-Tech next and try stealing the other businesses out from under your bodyguards. My sources say that Andrei has already been moving in on the illegal street businesses Winter and Weston are in charge of. They've been spending a lot of time in Chicago instead of monitoring things in Texas. You know, they have untrained employees and someone needed to strengthen that."

"Nice, Dmitri. Now you're trying to get me out of Chicago?"

"It's as good a time as any. Andrei isn't stupid. After tonight's display by Storm and Zin, I'd say Andrei's interest in owning you has just become priority. You will not be able to defy his orders and threats, Aspen. He can use you to control Storm, and his team."

"I don't plan on doing that. I don't want Storm, Winter, Zin, Weston, and York to get hurt because of me. But I can ensure that they keep their businesses and their livelihood striving. After all, we knew this was a possibility when we started planning this takedown. It will all work out. Worst scenario, I'll leave Chicago and head to Texas. I've got friends there, too."

"What are you going to do about Andrei? He wants you. Will want you even more knowing that Storm and Zin have feelings for you."

"They don't have feelings for me. They were proving a point. Showing me how weak I am and how incapable I am of dealing with men like Andrei. I was planning on staying in Chicago for another week or two. Then I'll be heading back to Texas."

"Good. You're safer there, and maybe even working for Storm and them. It seems they may have some deep exterminating to do in Pro-Tech Industries."

Aspen couldn't believe that Andrei had people working within the company to sabotage the business.

"Sounds like the only way to help them now is to take on the job and eliminate the threats."

"If anyone can do that, it's you. Then maybe if you resolve all this, you can seriously think about living a little? Maybe take me up on that trip around the world on my yacht?" Dmitri teased.

How badly she wished some other men were making a similar offer. But now she knew how they really felt about her. There were no intimate feelings, only obligation keeping them nearby.

"We'll see, Dmitri."

"Ah, so your answer gives me hope. You call me if you need anything. And watch your ass. Andrei will call upon you for a meeting to make his demands. Don't let him get you alone. The thought of his hands on you enrages me."

"I'll have to handle whatever he dishes out. Saving Pro-Tech and everything Storm and them have achieved is priority. Plus my brother's business is at stake as well as their friends from Liberty Construction and Development. I have no choice. I'll need to do whatever it is Andrei asks for while I'm cleaning house for Pro-Tech."

Chapter 3

"You must be losing your mind. Holy shit, Aspen, I can't believe all of this happened at the party last night. What are you going to do?"

"No big deal, India. I had it under control and knew sooner or later that Andrei was going to confront me. You had your own eye candy to enjoy. How was the blond anyway?" Aspen asked as she took a sip from her sparkling water. She was trying not to let on to the fact that her life was in danger and that she was working this angle to save her brother and her bodyguards' businesses. They were sitting at a table in LaFonte, a French restaurant a few blocks from the office in downtown.

"He was pretty good actually. Wanted me to stay today but I got this odd vibe. I don't know. I don't think he was totally up front with what exactly he does for a living."

Aspen chuckled. "I'm sure you were up front when you told him you make over four hundred thousand a year and have enough money saved to live an elaborate lifestyle for the next five lives."

"Of course not. Then he would use me for my money besides my body. No way."

"Well there you go. So will you see him again?"

India smiled. "Perhaps," she replied and Aspen laughed. India leaned forward. "How about you? How hard was it to not tear Zin's clothes off when he kissed you like that?"

"Hard. But that's not exactly the way I imagined one of them kissing me for the very first time. It makes me so angry to know that Zin at least feels something. They've always treated me like a little sister, thanks to Porter. But it's so strange. Like I've told you a thousand times before, India. I get this feeling, this strong, deep sensation like an invisible bond between me and the five of them. They're the only ones who seem to affect me in any way. I mean, Andrei had me by the throat and was threatening me, and I swear I was almost numb to the sensations. But Storm, Winter, York, Zin, and Weston can just look at me and get a reaction."

She played with the fork by her salad plate.

"Maybe they really do have feelings for you and are just fighting them?"

"No, Storm proved what was really going on last night," she said and explained what happened.

India leaned back and looked angry as she shook her head. "That's just fucked up. No wonder you're living on the edge right now, Aspen. That must have hurt. Especially since you want them so desperately."

"I don't want them. I get it now. I know I'm destined for loneliness. It's just what my life will always be like. No one. No man has the ability to get beyond this wall I have around my heart."

"That's not true. There must be someone out there you're meant to be with and fall in love with."

"I had to force myself to learn how to not feel. Condition myself to hold back and not give all of me to anything or anyone. Now here I am thinking about five men who I can't have, who obviously don't want me, and I feel like crap. How could they get to me like this when I know where my fate lies?"

"Sweetie, have you noticed the two guards that are stationed around the room? The same men who were at your penthouse when I picked you up this morning? Storm and his team care about you."

"But nothing can happen between us. Not when they see me as their sister. They proved this is all out of loyalty and obligation."

"I think it's more than that. I think they don't want to put you in any danger. They're not exactly running legitimate businesses. They have ties to the Russian mob, and they have enemies. Perhaps they don't want you placed into that type of danger?"

"I think last night proved that I can pretty much put myself in danger without their connections or business associates."

India laughed. "What would you have done if Andrei tried to make you leave with him?"

Aspen looked at her best friend and held her gaze very seriously. "I would have killed him the moment I had the chance."

"Excuse me, ladies, but the four gentlemen at the bar would like to buy you both a drink. Your choice." The waiter interrupted and both Aspen and India turned to see the four very attractive businessmen staring at them and raising their drink glasses. One of them was turned sideways and Aspen couldn't see his face.

India gave a small wave and then looked at the waiter. "We'll take a bottle of your 2007 Sassicaia Cabernet please. Oh, and thank the gentleman for us will ya, doll," India said without missing a beat as she ordered the two-hundred-dollar bottle of wine from Tuscany, Italy.

"Are you out of your mind?" Aspen asked as India winked at the men across the way.

"Nope. If they don't bat an eye at the price, then maybe I'll get their numbers. If they do, then we don't give them a second glance."

"Not me. Don't involve me in one of your testing charades. I don't know why you just can't take a man at face value. Why do you need to analyze him so much before committing?"

"I need to know a man wants me and this body and not my money. You have your ways of weaning through the bad ones and I have my ways. Which by the way, you haven't hooked up with anyone in like forever. What's with that? You can't tell me that Big Dave does it for you."

Aspen chuckled at the mention of Big Dave, the extra thick long dildo Aspen had purchased a few years back. India and her joked around about the name and the device, and especially when Aspen turned down offers of sex from real men. Aspen had a hard time with the intimacy and physical touching during sex. She could never really give up control and just let go no matter how much she wanted to. Her first lover was in college and truly just an excuse to get rid of her virginity and try to gain back some control and empowerment over her body. Thank God the men who had abducted her hadn't been successful in raping her and selling her off. She would surely have died.

Her second attempt at another near disastrous encounter was with Billy. He was such a sweet, compassionate man but when it came to sex, he just didn't have what it took to satisfy her. It was literally one time and they never saw one another again.

Aspen watched as the waiter brought over the bottle of wine, showed India the bottle, then opened it. She went through the motions of examining the cork, sniffing the glass of wine, and then sipping the small bit. She nodded and the waiter poured them both the glasses of wine then set the bottle on the table in a holder.

Aspen thought back on three years ago and her third attempt at sex. She was drunk, hoping intoxication would weaken her defenses and resolve at India's place during a huge party she had. The guy was gorgeous, wealthy, very muscular and charismatic. She thought this was finally it, a man capable of breaking down her defenses and bringing her the moment of pleasure she heard about and read about in magazines and talking to India. But once again, her inability to let go, to give in and allow a man to deeply connect to her, failed. So, she gave up. She purchased Big Dave and hadn't bothered having sex with anyone.

"Okay, sweetie, there are four of them heading over here. You choose first or they can choose for us. Maybe Big Dave won't be getting any action tonight, but two of these men will," India said as the four men approached.

Aspen felt her heart race and pound inside her chest. India had a lot more confidence when it came to flirting. But as Aspen looked over the four men, one of them stood out immediately as someone she had seen before.

"Aspen Brooks, I thought that was you," he said, as he moved really close and eyed her body over. The thick Russian accent couldn't be mistaken. India picked up on it, too. The other three put all their attention on her and barely on India. India's concerned expression was ignored a moment as she gave the once-over back to Iakov. The son of a bitch was one of Andrei's cousins. Now, getting a closer look at the other three as they took seats surrounding her and India, Aspen gained back that confidence and instant business attitude. Andrei wanted to place guards on her and watch her every move? Then she was going to act unaffected. What did it matter now? The deal was done. There was nothing she could do to change things or make it up to Andrei. Besides, she didn't trust the man to keep his hands off of her anyway.

"Iakov, meet my friend India. India, this is one of Andrei's cousins. I presume your friends here are also on the payroll?" Aspen asked and Iakov smiled. He winked at India and didn't bother with any introductions.

Instead he looked Aspen over again and licked his lower lip, holding her gaze intently.

"Seems you've gone and pissed off my cousin." She started to speak but he cut her off. "And for some reason he still likes you and wants to talk."

"Talk?" she asked, not believing him at all.

Iakov reached for her hand and covered it with his. He leaned closer to whisper so she would only hear him and not India or the others. Not that it mattered. The others were flirting with India and totally trying to get her to give them her number.

His cold, hard hand covered her hand that was on her thigh.

"You have something he wants, or at least an ability to get it. Lose your friends who are on their way over here, and I'll call you within the hour with a location to meet at." He winked and then stood up just as Storm's bodyguards approached the table. They probably had to call the guys first and ask what they should do. Especially since Aspen was sure they witnessed the exchange between her, India, and these four men and the bottle of wine.

The four men walked away and the guards asked if India and Aspen were okay.

"Of course we are," Aspen said and then reached for the wine glass. She downed the wine and looked at India.

"I think our plans for the afternoon have changed."

She saw India's concerned expression as the guards walked away and knew that India would help her lose the security guys. This was something she needed to face, or she may never get Andrei off her ass. Ignoring a mob boss would get her killed.

* * * *

"She'll never agree to meet me here at my home. Text her to be at Almafi's at five," Andrei told Iakov.

"Almafi's? Aren't you meeting Sotoro there?" Iakov asked Andrei.

"I am, but she won't know anything about that. I don't expect Aspen to stay long. Once I tell her what I need from her and how she's going to assist me then we'll be done. She'll hightail it outta there quickly."

"What is it that you need her to do, and do you think she'll actually do it?"

"Oh, she'll come through. Her brother's life and his friends' lives depend upon it."

* * * *

Aspen's phone rang as she got out of the cab outside of Almafi's restaurant. She kind of felt badly for losing Storm's security detail. It also made her feel a bit naked not having the gun power nearby, but she needed to do this. Besides, this place was always so crowded. Too many people around to not notice her arrival or see that she was meeting Iakov. What she hadn't expected was to see Demyan there nor for him to greet her. His eyes widened and a small smirk took over his expression. She on the other hand felt on edge a bit more than a few moments ago.

"Ah, so we meet again. You never returned my calls this week, Aspen. I'm offended."

She knew that he did business with Andrei Renoke. In fact, Demyan was one of his main associates with family ties to a Russian organization centuries old. She wasn't trying to piss off such powerful individuals. She was only seeking some revenge, though minor, to alleviate the constant pain of bad memories she felt from her past. Scoring the construction job was huge. She needed to be smart, and to use her assets to save her from any potential harm.

She smiled at Demyan. "You knew I wouldn't answer your calls. I told you, Demyan, I don't date men I work with."

"How about just sleep with them?" he asked, pulling her closer and letting his hand roam over her hips. At first she was going to pull away but then she realized that he was frisking her. He was checking to see if she was carrying.

Iakov approached and held his hand out. She knew he wanted her to give him her purse to check that, too. She did and he gave her a wink, looked her body over, and then checked her purse. At this point Demyan released her slowly but not completely. He turned her around and placed his hands on her hips as Iakov walked ahead of them through the crowded restaurant.

It was actually kind of weird how no one even glanced at them, or looked to watch as the men frisked hr. It was obviously not such a foreign sight.

She calmed her breathing best she could, considering she was feeling pretty much on edge. The further they walked, the less and less people were around them. As they made it to the back hallway she realized that she may not be quite prepared for Andrei and this meeting. What could he possibly want from her for him to call this meeting? Was he intending on threatening her more? Perhaps giving her a beating? Maybe forcing himself on her? She didn't think so. One thing she learned from studying Andrei for so long was that he was a planner. He never reacted on impulse and when he made a move or an attack it was out of the blue and unexpected.

No, he definitely had something up his sleeve and the fact that she was still alive said a lot.

Iakov opened the door and there was Gary Sparks, the CEO of the company she worked for, and he didn't look too good at all.

She looked to Andrei, who leaned against the desk with a snifter of vodka in his hand.

"Ah, there she is. We've been waiting for you, Aspen."

He stood straighter, placed his drink down, and Iakov gave her a small shove toward Andrei. She gave Iakov a dirty look and Demyan chuckled.

"What's going on?" she asked, but Andrei eyed her over, took her hand, and brought it to his lips and kissed the top.

"You look gorgeous as usual, Ms. Brooks." He held her gaze, his expression from smug to a look of power.

"Iakov, a drink for Aspen please."

He released her hand and led her to the chair in front of his desk and beside Gary Sparks.

"What are you doing here?" she asked Gary. He looked her over and then cleared his throat as he looked at Andrei.

"I was just negotiating the sale of Sparks Industries. Seems I'm going to retire a lot earlier then I originally planned," her boss told her and she was shocked. Somehow Andrei had bought out Gary Sparks's business. This was a business many people were interested in taking over, including her brother Porter, Storm and his team, as well as associates of theirs who had similar businesses in New York and

Texas. Galvin Quarters had been negotiating the sale for years. They'd had Storm, Winter, and the gang introduce him to Gary two years ago. What kind of game was Andrei playing?

"I don't understand. I mean you haven't mentioned wanting to retire or sell the business."

"Things change, Aspen," Gary said and then stood up.

"Circumstances change. I already own a large number of similar companies around Chicago. By purchasing Sparks Industries, I gain a monopoly over the industry," Andrei said and took a sip of his drink.

Aspen understood what was going on here. This had to do with his own sense of revenge and power. Andrei wanted to take over Nicolai Merkovicz's territory, and that was some serious dangerous moves on his part.

Aspen sat back and thought about what was happening and how she had to keep her mouth shut and not let on to how much she knew about the Russian mob families that ruled Chicago and elsewhere. Nicolai was not the kind of man to mess with, nor was his family. From her understanding, there were men, family members, embedded in Andrei's organization and he didn't even know it. This was too much to digest.

"So why did you ask me to meet you here? I'm not a partner in Sparks Industries," she said.

"I'm your boss now, Aspen, and there are certain things required of you in your new position."

"New position? I don't think so."

"He owns the contracts now, Aspen. There's no legal way out of this," Gary said as Iakov motioned for him to leave the room. Aspen watched with concern.

"You are going to be the new CEO of my company. I have a major project I want you to work on in taking over another small business I think will be a great new avenue for my new company."

She stared at him and he smiled.

"You're going to help me get the information I need to sabotage Pro-Tech Industries and take it over," he said and smirked.

Her gasp was so loud as she sat forward, shocked at him. "Are you out of your mind? That's Storm Jones's company. Those guys are not men to mess with. There is no way I'm doing that. Besides, I quit. You can take the contract and shove it up your—"

Demyan yanked her hair back, making her slide half off the chair. She screamed and grabbed onto the arms of the chair so she wouldn't fall.

"You don't seem to get the man's orders, Aspen. You are going to do this. If you don't, your good friend India is going to experience exactly what you did when you were seventeen. Except she won't be saved by anyone. She'll be sold to the highest bidder as a sex slave and shipped out of the country. She is used goods, though, the way she fucks around so much, but can still grab a pretty penny."

The tears stung Aspen's eyes. India would never survive that. Aspen didn't even want to think about these men doing that to her best friend.

"Why are you doing this? Because of the construction job? I'll get you something else. Something bigger than Pro-Tech Industries," she said.

Andrei walked closer and cupped her chin. "My sweet, sweet Aspen. You will do as I say or India will disappear tonight."

He leaned down and kissed her deeply and all she could do was let him as she fell under the strong arm of the Russian mob that now owned her once again against her will.

When he finally released her, Iakov released her hair and Demyan was there to pull her up from the chair. He cupped her cheek and stared down into her eyes.

"We're going to make a good team, and perhaps not only in business." He ran the palm of his hand from her cheek to her neck then over her breast.

She pushed his hand away and he gripped her and got between her legs, causing them to spread open, nearly ripping her skirt.

He held her neck and face in between his hands and stared down into her eyes.

"Men have died for less. Behave and do as we say and no one will get hurt." He leaned forward and sniffed her hair. His lips and tongue collided against her ear and neck and she squirmed under his hold.

"Let her be, Demyan. There'll be plenty of time for that. She's ours now and she knows it. Iakov, show Aspen out. She needs some time to digest her new position. Oh, and don't think about sharing it with your bodyguards. No one will know your new title. For now. You'll do what we want or your brother and his friends will find themselves in need of medical attention if not an undertaker."

Iakov showed her out and she felt her body shaking with fear. These men were criminals of the worse kind and now she was going to be forced to help them destroy men who she desired but could not have in that way. As they made their way through the hallway, she was so upset she nearly missed the sight of Victor Sotoro. What the hell was he doing here? It had to be to see Andrei, but why? Was he going to be forced to help take down Pro-Tech Industries, too? Or was Dmitri correct, and Sotoro was working for Andrei already and helping to take Storm and the team out of commission?

She wondered if Storm, Winter, and the guys knew they'd made such enemies. As she exited the restaurant, anger began to build inside of her. She was as good as dead anyway. Why not go out in a bang and clean out the spies in Pro-Tech Industries, while also working to enhance another security firm much larger than all of these? If she was now being pulled into mob-related operations, she could get killed. Why not make it worth it?

Andrei wanted her to be a player in his little game. Then she was going to be the best player of them all.

* * * *

"What the hell is going on, Storm? Aspen hasn't answered any of my calls," Porter demanded as he stood in his hotel room in Germany. His buddies were all there waiting for him to make this call and get word on Aspen. They were all concerned.

"She ditched the security team we placed on her. I've got men trying to track her down," Storm told him.

"How the hell does my sister ditch two of your best security men?"

Porter's buddies—Piers, Wren, Reid, and Silas—smirked.

"I'm sure my sister helped," Silas said in the background, speaking of India. Porter knew India and Aspen were best friends. They helped one another get through some pretty tough times.

"She's more resourceful than any of us, including you, Porter, have given her credit for. I told you what was going on. I just hope she's not alone with Andrei," Storm said.

"You and me both. He's wanted her since day one. He's been out for our territory for years and taking Aspen as a teen was a strategic move on his part. He should have been taken out for it," Porter said.

"Yeah well that wasn't in the plan now was it? She definitely knows that he's the one who had her abducted. I won't let that need for revenge cost her her life. We've spoken to Dmitri and claimed her our property," Storm informed him.

Porter was silent. He knew that these men were in love with his sister. They'd denied those feelings to protect her and keep her out of this life, a life maybe they were all destined to be involved in. But Aspen had been through enough years ago. She had a bull's-eye on her forehead and the only way to get rid of that bull's-eye was to get rid of Andrei.

"I hope Andrei abides by this move and stays clear of her," Porter told Stone.

"He'd better. Andrei, Demyan, and Iakov have no business doing anything in Texas. This is our territory."

"And if he uses this as an opportunity to try and take over what you have in Chicago?"

"I'll deal with that when the time comes. Aspen is our priority, and building up our resources in Texas is where we need to focus our energy."

"And what about Sotoro? I feel out of the loop being in Germany for the month. Any details on him and the concern that he's working his way into your Chicago connections?"

"No, but I'm sure Nicolai is all over that. Remember when he contacted me about confronting Sotoro so there wouldn't be a war?"

"Well if things like this situation keep popping up, that's exactly what there's going to be. Bloodshed over who will ultimately run that territory. You know that you're risking losing some control by bringing Aspen to Texas and remaining there? I'm bringing the whole team with me, too. I won't let Andrei get his claws into Aspen."

"Neither will we. We'll see you in a few days."

"Protect her, Storm. We'll see you soon."

Porter disconnected the call and looked at the guys. Piers, Ren, Reid, and Silas. They'd been his team since serving in the military and came from similar family backgrounds like him and Aspen. They were a wild bunch, never really learning how to settle down and live life like regular civilians. They each had a specialty, an ability that landed them a lot of private contracts for everything from security to applying pressure to get individuals to pay up. But they only did those jobs in between working for both Liberty Construction and Development and working for Pro-Tech Industries.

"How is Aspen?" Piers asked him.

Porter ran his hands through his hair as he told him and the guys about what Storm knew and filled him in on.

"Sounds like she's hiding shit. You're going to have to get it out of her as soon as we get to Salvation," Ren said.

"No shit. But she's changed over the last few years. I should have seen this coming. I should have recognized the signs," Porter told them.

"Of what? That she wanted to seek revenge? That she figured out that Andrei was responsible for her abduction years ago? Then what? You weren't ready to talk to her about her father and the past," Silas stated.

"You think I should now?" Porter asked, knowing that only his team knew the details of the family ties to the Russian mob. Surely Andrei couldn't know. The secret was something he had come to know by accident.

"I think it may be necessary to help her make the right decisions," Reid told him.

"The right decision about what?"

"About letting Andrei control her. If she knew the truth, she may be making some different choices."

"Like what, Reid?" Porter asked.

"Like accepting a part of her heritage that's been kept a secret from her since her birth. Your sister has more than proven her capabilities and strength. You need to tell her the truth. She's obviously done her own investigating into Andrei. It's only fair for her to know," Silas said.

"I'll think about it. I just know, from what we've heard, that Andrei wants her but for what besides his woman, I don't know. But knowing the man, and his capabilities, I'm fearful he'll succeed and I'll lose her forever."

Chapter 4

She tried to pull on the sweater to hide the bruising on her upper arm caused by Demyan in Andrei's office. But it was too late when Storm, Winter, Zin, York, and Weston opened the front door to her penthouse apartment.

"What the hell?" she asked, stunned at their audacity.

"Where the fuck did you go? Why did you lose your security guards?" Storm demanded to know as they piled into her living room.

"First of all, what gives you the right to break into my home uninvited? What if I was entertaining someone?" she snapped as York approached and raised an eyebrow at her.

"You haven't dated anyone since that guy from New York you had living here," he said. She gave him a dirty look but then Weston grabbed her hand.

"What's this? How did this happen?" he asked.

Busted.

She tried pulling away from him. "I don't know. I banged it," she lied.

"Banged it my ass. There's fucking finger marks on it," he said, twisting her arm a little to get a better look.

"Aspen, did you meet up with Andrei at his restaurant LaFonte?" Winter asked her.

"That's none of your business."

"Fuck it isn't!" Zen yelled out. They were all gathered around her now. Weston released her hand and cupped her neck and cheek. She felt his other hand go to her waist.

Weston Galloway was tall with dark brown hair and deep green eyes. He was very trim and muscular, dressed casually in his designer black T-shirt and blue jeans.

"Baby, you need to tell us what went down in that meeting. You can't handle this alone."

So many things went through her head. How badly she wanted to trust them, to confide in them and tell them that she was doing this to save them, her brother, and India. But she couldn't. They would place her in hiding or something and freak out and then Andrei would succeed in taking over all their companies and territory she'd just recently learned these men occupied. So they weren't involved with the Mafia in a minor way. They were knee-deep.

"I am alone. I get that now. Storm and Zin proved to me where you all really stand and how alone I am in this life for however long it is."

Weston reached back and cupped her head.

"You're not alone. You have us, Porter, and India."

"I don't need to hear it. You all made it clear to me. I'm fine, and I'm working things out with Andrei. He hasn't asked for much. Just my company," she said and started to pull away.

Weston's hands gripped her firmer, keeping her in place.

"That fucking bastard can't have you," he said as the others made similar statements.

"Don't worry, I don't need to spread my legs just yet." She pulled from Weston's hold. She knew she sounded bitchy, but what they did to her, how Storm and even Zin kissed her obviously to prove a point was still fresh on her mind.

She saw Weston look at Storm and Winter as if he wanted to say something and then Storm shook his head.

"That offer is still on the table with working for us. We're still in charge of keeping you safe, and Porter said you're not answering his calls. We all think you need to go back to Texas and work at Pro-Tech until this shit blows over with Andrei," Storm told her.

"Oh really? Is that what you all decided?" she asked, knowing she couldn't come off too easily about this even though it was her plan to return and weed out the shits infiltrating their company.

"Yes. Porter will be returning from Europe this week and expects you to be at the company. He's worried, just like the rest of us are."

"Oh, I'm sure he is, Storm. I'm certain you explained how weak I am and how much trouble I got myself into?"

"Aspen, just accept the protection. We know how to handle men like Andrei," Zin told her.

She shot him a look. "I'm sure you do. I'll think about it. Considering that I have work to do with Clarence as well in Texas, I'll see if I have the time to retrain your employees."

"You will have the time. I spoke with Dmitri today and your services will no longer be needed with the project except on a minor level leaving you plenty of time to work for us," Winter informed her.

"What? How could you? Why would Dmitri agree to this?"

"He had no choice. We've claimed ownership of you for your protection. Andrei can't touch you or contact you without our consent, and that isn't going to happen," Storm told her.

"And if I deny this ownership of protection I'm assuming is some sort of Mafia rule," she snapped at him with her arms crossed in front of her. She was planning on this and so was Andrei, the slimy bastard.

"We'll make your life a living hell. All of your assets will be frozen leaving you no means of escape or available resources to plan an escape. Now that we know what you're capable of, we're ready to take the necessary precautions," Weston said.

Zin and York smiled.

"Welcome to Pro-Tech Industries. Pack your bags, sweetheart, the plane leaves tonight," York said. She gave them the best dirty look she could when really she was relieved the plan worked.

She would save these men, her brother, and India, and she would destroy Andrei once and for all. Even if it cost her the love of five men and her life.

* * * *

Weston and York sat on either side of Aspen on the private jet. Weston thought she looked so tired, but every time she began to doze off she would jerk awake.

"Lean on me. I don't mind, Aspen," Weston told her. He hoped she would because he loved the scent of her perfume, and the softness of her body leaning against his. He had this overwhelming feeling of protectiveness over her, and it only seemed to ease slightly when she was right nearby.

He glanced at York, who turned to face her.

"Still having trouble sleeping at night?"

She ignored his question, an obvious show of her refusal to discuss anything personal with any of them. Storm's actions were misconstrued by her, with help from Storm of course. He'd lied to hide his true feelings and completely insulted her. Now she believed they didn't care about her and that she was more of a job. That was a lie. She was everything they ever wanted and couldn't have. Though he was thinking just maybe, they could.

"They have things that you can take for that. Nothing addictive, maybe take the edge off so you can get a good night's sleep," York pushed.

Aspen shot her head up and looked at York. "Is that what you do? Take drugs to forget about the things you did while serving? Is that how you deal with being part of the Russian mob?" she asked with attitude.

"Don't push me, Aspen. You're in no position to gain more enemies."

"Oh really. Like I give a shit? I think I'm in a great position to gain more enemies. Why not? I'm as good as dead anyway."

She turned away and began to finger through some fashion magazine. Weston covered her hand and grabbed it. She stilled under his control but didn't look up.

"We know you're scared but this is the best way to protect you and keep Andrei from hurting you. You don't know what kind of monster he really is."

"Oh really? You don't think I know anything about mob bosses? You know what? Maybe you're right. You want to teach me, since the five of you seem to be listed under the title *made men*."

"Don't push your luck, Aspen. You're under our control now. What we say and order you to do, you will do," Storm interrupted.

She sat forward in the seat, pulling away from Weston.

"I get what you really feel about me. I get that I'm an obligation, so back off. I'll work at the damn company and clean it up so it functions better than it ever has before. My personal life"—she looked at Weston and York—"and my sleeping habits are none of your business."

She sat back and closed her eyes. Weston looked at Storm, who stared at her and appeared about ready to bolt out of his seat. But he was holding back. He was fighting the urge they all had to claim Aspen completely and protect her with their bodies, their hearts, and souls as well as their connections and power. But still they couldn't. Not with Andrei wanting to cause her harm, and not with all the changes coming in the family operations. No, they had to bite their tongues and see who made the next move amongst the bosses. Then they could all be involved with a blood war.

* * * *

It had been four days since arriving back in Salvation. It took thirty minutes to drive into the city to Pro-Tech Industries, and Aspen already had a list of employees she was going to further investigate. The men gave her total control of decision making, hiring, and firing employees and how she handled all aspects of her job. The employees learned fast that she expected respect. She sat in the small office the men had set up for her and she looked over the training manuals and testing programs set up to monitor employees who took the initial calls from potential clients. From there she began to rewrite the manuals and offer advice on the types of questions phone reps needed to ask and then the follow-up interview process.

Some of the employees argued that there wasn't enough time to conduct the whole interview process and they lost potential customers because of that. She ensured them that any potential customers they lost who didn't have the patience or acceptance to answer the questions and provide legitimate documentation were clients Pro-Tech Industries didn't want or need. There were plenty of private investigators out there sleazy enough to only care about the money and nothing else.

She took a deep breath and released it, feeling her head begin to pound from the lack of sleep. She should be sleeping perfectly in the king-size bed, and especially with the cool country air filtering through her bedroom window at night. But she couldn't. She kept thinking about the men in the house, how they made her move in with them, and of course the moment she drifted off to sleep she had nightmares.

Weston heard her one night and knocked on her door and asked if she was okay. She blew him off, and last night Zin heard her and she denied there was any problem.

She should feel safer with the five Navy SEALs in the same house with guns galore around the place. But the strength of those memories and the fact that she should have died seemed to overpower anything else.

Aspen looked at the list she'd begun to devise then pulled out the iPad mini and sent the list and information to Dmitri. She then sent a bogus report to Andrei but also asked for a few of his inside people planted in the firm. She figured what the hell. Just like most people, she was a lot more brazen over e-mail then in person. Maybe he would actually give up a name or two. That would give her a greater start to her list of suspects already. She hit send and then quickly deleted her mail and the bogus account she set up then reached down and placed the iPad mini back into her bag.

She was yawning and covering her mouth when she heard the knock on her door.

Zin walked into the room and she couldn't help but react to him. Her heart began to beat faster, a smile began to form on her face, and she quickly hid it and looked down at her desk, placing her fingers on the keyboard.

He looked incredible in his dark blue polo shirt and black dress pants. No wonder the majority of female employees who worked there drooled over the men.

"Are you just about ready to leave?" Zin asked her. His blue eyes zeroed in on her blouse, and as she adjusted her position in the chair, she noticed how the collar parted, revealing more cleavage than she intended and the pearl necklace was lost inside her blouse between her breasts.

"Sure. Let me just log out of here and grab my things." She typed on the keyboard and then stood up and gathered some files she wanted to look over as well as the thumb drive with the material she was using to rewrite the training manual.

She walked around the desk and toward the filing cabinet she'd set up and as she turned to set the items into her bag, Zin stood in her way.

She stared up into his handsome face. His blue eyes held her gaze and he inhaled as if he was taking in her scent. It did something to her, aroused her, but then she reminded herself that he had been testing her and showing her weakness to a man's attempt at seduction. That was the only reason why he kissed her that night on the balcony.

"Steak good for dinner tonight? Weston left a little earlier to get things started."

She nodded her head as he reached up and ran his fingers along her neck. She shivered from the intimate touch as he zeroed in on her breasts and gently, slowly pulled the necklace from confinement.

Zin slid his fingers down the string of pearls and softly feathered over her cleavage to set them over her blouse causing the material to pull together and hide her skin.

"How about a little wine with dinner tonight? Maybe it will relax you a bit," he suggested, and she stepped back and reached for her bag and her purse.

"I'm pretty tired. So much so that a glass of wine might do me in."

"It may make for a good night's sleep," he said as she headed toward the door, him turning the lights off behind her.

She knew what he was hinting at and she wasn't going to get into this with Zin, with any of them.

"I'm fine, Zin," she said.

He said good night to the secretary, who was gathering her things, and a few other stragglers, including one woman Pamela, whom Aspen had already added to her watch list. Pamela's eyes landed on Zin and then his hand as Zin kept it at Aspen's lower back as he guided her out of the office toward the elevators.

"Good night, Zin," Pamela called out. He gave a wave and Aspen harrumphed under her breath. It was obvious by the woman's expression and eyes that she had a thing for Zin and was jealous of Aspen. Definitely one woman to keep an eye on and never turn her back on either.

They got into the elevator, and as Zin pressed the button for the lobby, Aspen caught sight of Pamela staring at her as she spoke on the cell phone she put to her ear.

"What's that expression for?" Zin asked, crossing his arms and looking at her as he stood slightly in front of her. He was always in a protective stance. Like her own shield of armor.

"Nothing, just noticing the way Pamela looks at you."

He raised one eyebrow up at her in that sexy way that Zin knew turned women on. She would be lying if she said it didn't affect her.

"One of your regulars?" she shot back at his cocky expression. He stepped forward and she instinctually stepped back, her rear hitting the wall of the elevator. One of his hands went to her waist and the other against the wall over her shoulder.

"Jealous?" he challenged.

She chuckled but it came out as an odd sound that gave away her frazzled state. Not many men could frazzle her. Zin obviously could.

"No."

He pressed his body against hers and whispered close to her lips "Liar."

The elevator stopped and the doors opened but he didn't move. She raised one eyebrow up at him and he let the hand that was above her shoulder slide down her arm to her hand, clasping his and hers together.

He pulled her along and she had no choice but to follow him through the lobby and past the security cameras as well as the security desk. The men working there smiled wide and said good night. It was in that moment she realized why Zin was doing this, making a show of possession. Those same men had flirted with her the first few days. In fact one of them mentioned having drinks this Friday after work and her joining them. As they walked out the front entrance, the black SUV was sitting there running.

"Jealous much?" she asked as he opened the door and there were Storm and Winter. Both Weston and York were probably both preparing dinner back at the estate. She climbed up into the SUV, her blouse obviously parting again as Storm and Winter looked directly at her chest.

She sat back against the seat, placed her bags on the floor, and then adjusted her blouse.

"All set?" Storm asked. Zin mumbled a "yes." Then Storm began to drive out of the parking lot.

* * * *

Zin was feeling pretty damn angry and hell yeah, jealous. Those fucking guys downstairs that worked the security desk had been talking about Aspen since day one. They were talking about her body, how hot she was, and even had the nerve to flirt with her and ask her to meet them for drinks. They were some of the best guys they had working for them but he would fire their asses if need be.

He completely forgot about how annoyed Aspen looked after Pamela said good night to him and flirted. Aspen thought he had slept with Pamela. He wanted to kiss Aspen in the elevator and nearly did when the doors opened. Then he completely forgot about all of it as she waved good night to the guys and they checked out her ass and all smiled and waved good-bye.

"I wasn't the least bit jealous. I just don't think any of those guys are your type at all," he told her and she turned to look at him. His remark grabbed Storm and Winter's attention, too.

"Really? Like you know what my type is? I could say the same about Pamela. She's definitely not your type."

"Why would you say that?" he countered, turning to look at her. She was so fucking beautiful. Even riled up, he felt his dick trying to push through his pants.

"Too small up top and hardly even has an ass. You've always been a tits and ass kind of guy," she retorted, and Winter chuckled.

"Yeah, well those guys aren't your type at all either. They live to watch sporting events and they don't hit dance clubs like that guy Jester you were living with."

She gasped. "Jester had a great body. You jealous because he had amazing, sexy moves on a dance floor?"

"I can dance. I just prefer nice and slow. You know, while my hands are exploring a woman's big tits and ass."

She glared at him and crossed her arms and turned to look away.

He cursed under his breath as Storm continued to drive.

"What ever happened between you and Jester anyway? It was like he appeared out of nowhere. You were with him every waking minute, and then he disappeared. Where did he go?" Winter asked her even though they knew where he went. Back to New York to work for some accounting firm.

"It didn't work out."

"How come?" Zin asked her.

She looked at him and gave him the once-over. "He didn't do it for me anymore," she stated.

He knew she was trying to rile him and damn was she doing a great job at that. But before he could come up with a reply, the SUV stopped and she opened the door. Storm was out and helping her down. She reached for her bags and headed inside with Winter holding the front door open for her.

"What the fuck is going on?" Storm asked Zin. Zin ran his fingers through his hair.

"I'm losing my mind. I can't take not touching her, kissing her, and wanting her. The fucking guys at work are talking about her body, her sweet personality, and it's killing me."

"You need to hold off."

"Fuck holding off. If something happens between us, then it does and that's it. I want her. I want to hold her, comfort her when she wakes with those damn nightmares. How can you and the others stay out of her room when I know you hear her crying and moaning in pain? She remembers that night. She relives her abduction every fucking night and sleeps with all the lights on in the room. Not even a fucking nightlight."

He turned around and headed into the house. How the fuck was he going to get through dinner?

* * * *

Aspen didn't know what came over her. She was being bitchy, trying to cause a fight with Zin because she was jealous. That Pamela woman wanted him.

"Hey, how are you doing?" York asked her as he came out of the kitchen with a dishtowel hanging from the waist of his jeans.

He looked so good, her heart immediately began to pound and her mouth nearly watered from the sight of him. All male, muscles, and a tattoo on his arm that made her want to explore his body to find out if there were more tattoos elsewhere.

"She's fine," Zin said for her.

She swung her head to look at him and the man appeared crazed and angry, and it was directed at her.

Behind him was Storm looking just as pissed. Winter and Weston stood by the entrance to the kitchen in a dead stare.

Zin began to walk by her.

"What's your problem?" she said, snapping at him, and it was too late when she saw the change in his eyes. She stepped back and he was on her in a flash.

Her one retreating step was halted by a single strong arm that wrapped around her waist and pulled her against Zin's chest.

"You're my fucking problem," Zin said and then pressed his mouth over hers and began kissing her.

The tables turned quickly on her, making her head feel fuzzy, her body suddenly filled with overwhelming sensations. She felt every touch, every caress and shock to her system as Zin took complete control over her.

His tongue plunged into her mouth in exploration and possession. She gripped his shoulders and pulled at his polo shirt as her mind tried to decipher what the hell was happening here. She was confused, yet completely aroused and affected by his touch, his actions, and his dominance. But then came the reality of this. He didn't care for her in that way. He was teaching her a lesson. But what lesson was it? The old traditional belief that men overpowered women? Perhaps the misconception that women could be ultimately controlled by a man's dick? No, no fucking way. Not her. Not like this. She was in love with him, with *them* goddamn it!

She pulled from his mouth. The sound of his heavy breathing matched her own. His eyes looked wild and his face was red, tight, the muscles and veins standing out more so by his temples and neck as he strained to keep control.

"What the hell are you doing? Is this how you welcome your new female employees? You fuck them?" She spat her words at him.

She felt the palms of his hands glide under her skirt, lifting it and gripping her ass, squeezing as he simultaneously lifted her by her ass cheeks and pressed her hard against the wall a mere foot behind her.

She gasped and grabbed his shoulders as the feel of his belt and the material from his pants chaffed against her inner thighs.

"No. I don't fuck my female employees. The only woman I want to fuck is the one I've wanted to fuck for at least the last five years." He covered her mouth and kissed her again as his words sunk in. He wanted her? He desired her in that way? Was it just the macho, male mobster who wanted to claim a piece of ass and she was one woman he never could have because of her past, his loyalty to her brother, or simply because he was sexually attracted to her? Did she even care?

She realized very quickly as the sound of her panties tearing and the feel of his tongue plunging into her mouth took away any ability to talk.

She gasped as thick, hard fingers pressed against her very unusually wet pussy before they plunged up into her.

"Oh God!" she cried out, pulling from his lips. Zin suckled against her neck, rocked his hips in sync to his fingers as he thrust them into her. She felt his tongue, his lips, and his teeth against her sensitive skin and she moaned. She'd never felt anything like this before. Never.

"Open for me, Aspen. I know you want it. I know you feel exactly the way I do. I want you. I want to be inside of you. Tell me you feel it, too. Tell me you want it, damn you." He grunted and thrust his fingers, and she felt her body tighten. She felt something foreign, strange overpower all other feelings in her body and she feared letting go.

"Give it to him. Let go, Aspen, and give it to him now." Storm's strong voice surrounded her. She looked at him. She saw the arousal on his face, on Zin's face as Zin continued to pump his fingers up into her cunt.

Then the others were there. Winter, Weston, and York, and they all looked hungry. They all wanted her and the desire, the need overwhelmed her completely and she let go.

"Oh!" She screamed her release, shaking, rocking her pussy against Zin's thick, hard fingers as she screamed through the most amazing orgasm ever.

"That's it baby. Goddamn, Aspen, you look so fucking gorgeous when you come," Zin told her.

"She looks incredible, like an angel when she comes," York said, and she felt embarrassed. Suddenly like a fool for letting go like this. She tightened her thighs.

Zin pulled his fingers from her cunt and brought them to his mouth. He sucked the glistening cream off each finger. "Fucking delicious."

She felt her lips part and she stared at him in awe. Never in her life did she imagine feeling like this. The desire, the depth of emotion, the bond that was instantly there when she was around these men.

"Unbutton that blouse and show me what's mine," he ordered.

She didn't dare move. Her mind was trying to gain control of her body and what it wanted, which was for him to fuck her right here against the wall and fill her with cock so deep she couldn't speak or scream, only come like she just did over and over again.

"Do it now," he demanded as he reached under them, pressing her against the wall as he undid his pants.

"Zin."

"No. No fucking words of denial. No lies, no fucking games. I want you, you want me, just like the others. Now show me what belongs to me. To all of us."

"We want you. Always have," Storm admitted and she looked at each of the men as she reached for the buttons of her blouse with shaking fingers.

She opened her mouth to speak as she parted the blouse, and Winter helped to remove it from her body. She lifted her hips and felt the tip of Zin's cock at her the entrance to her pussy.

"I'm clean. I know you're on the pill. Tell me that you fucking want me right now, right here, baby," Zin said to her.

"How do you know I'm on the pill?" she found herself asking, stalling in an attempt to act nonchalant about this entire wild and crazy situation. But her voice shook and her body betrayed her as she pressed her wet pussy downward to get another feel of the tip of Zin's thick, hard cock.

Zin leaned forward and kissed the corner of her mouth on both sides and then trailed kisses along her neck.

"I know you've been on the pill since you were sixteen due to a doctor's recommendation. I know you prefer black thong panties over every other color because your lingerie drawer is filled with them. You're a size thirty-six double D, and I admit I've snuck into your bedroom and sniffed your pillow, ran my hands over your panties, and imagined cupping these breasts and fucking you while you screamed my name," he told her as he cupped her breast and pressed his cock slowly into her. She was so slick, so wet and ready for him, she moaned and allowed his control.

"That's it. God, baby, I've waited for-fucking-ever to make you mine."

She felt how hard and thick he was and gasped as he pushed his cock deeper into her cunt.

She locked gazes with him and he lowered his tongue to the cleavage of her breasts and licked between the crevice.

"Oh God, Zin. You feel so big."

"I am big," he said with confidence and then pressed deeper, working his thick cock into her tight folds.

"Fuck, baby, you're so fucking tight. I can't get all the way in. Let me in. Don't fight me."

"I'm not fighting you. It's been forever for me," she admitted.

He pulled out a little and then thrust a little deeper. She thought he might tear her pussy apart he was so thick and long.

"Oh God, Zin." She rocked her hips and pressed back against the wall.

"What do you mean forever?" Winter asked. "You were living with Jester less than a year ago."

She saw the jealousy in his eyes and the anger. It aroused her, turned her on, and lubricated her pussy.

"Jester was just a friend. He's gay, Winter. It was just an act to keep the men away from me."

A series of "whats" went through the room and Zin roared. "Are you fucking kidding me?"

Zin thrust his cock all the way in and she moaned.

As his entire body pressed against her and the wall, Zin locked gazes with her and she knew their relationship was never going to be the same again. With him buried deep inside of her, the whole world changed.

He kissed her on the mouth and took complete control over her body. He was possessing her, claiming her in the wildest, most erotic way. In and out he thrust his hips, filling her with cock and making her gasp for each breath. She ran her fingers through his hair, counterthrusting against his cock as he gripped her ass with both hands, spreading her ass cheeks and plunging into her at record speed. He was literally banging her against the wall and she'd never felt so wild and aroused in her entire life.

Her breasts bounced and she felt herself come again and again. The sound filled the room. Their pleasured comments about how wet she was and how turned on they were rumbled through her ears.

"Ours. We're making you all ours tonight. No other men ever again, Aspen. No one fucks this pussy, this ass but us ever again," Zin commanded and she felt his cock grow thicker and then his finger press over her puckered hole, wet from her cream, and penetrate her hole.

"Oh God, Zin!" she screamed and came from his words and his ministrations.

She was so utterly aroused by every sensation, every aspect of the way Zin took her like this. The way his muscular arms and fingers possessed her while his cock possessed her, too. The intensity of his facial expression, and the depth of his desires and emotions looked raw for all to see. And of course the others standing there surrounding them in that protective shield was what completed it all. She wasn't just making love with Zin. She was connecting with all of them on a deeper, more intimate level. She was beginning to penetrate that barrier she'd admired from afar and often wondered what it would feel like to be part of such a strong, unbreakable bond.

"Mine, Aspen. You're mine now and forever." Zin thrust into her, held himself deep, and came, convulsing, rocking, and moaning as he released his seed into her womb.

She hugged him tight, kissed his neck, his cheek, and then inhaled against his skin like she'd never done with any man she had sex with before because she knew this was different. This moment changed them all forever.

* * * *

Zin hugged Aspen to him as he calmed his breathing. He never expected making love to her would feel like this. He knew it would be special. Hell, he was madly in love with the woman and lusted for her for years. But this was so much more than any fantasy he ever had.

He stepped out of his pants, still holding her in his arms, and his cock still inside of her. He felt content like this. He felt like he protected her, made her a complete part of him. Never had he felt anything so deep and strong.

"Baby, that was incredible. I've waited so long for that. To be lost inside of you like this."

"Me, too," she whispered, slightly pulling back.

They locked gazes. "What are you saying?" he asked her and could tell she got uncomfortable and was being shy even after he'd just fucked her against the front entryway of their home, hopefully her home soon enough.

She glanced at the others and then nibbled her bottom lip.

"I guess I've kind of had a crush on all of you for quite some time."

Winter reached over and ran his knuckles along her cheek. "A crush, Aspen?"

"Well pretty much. I guess I wanted all of you, too. But then Storm pretty much said that you didn't feel the same way and that I was weak and controllable by a man. I figured you all didn't feel the same way."

"I didn't say that. I didn't mean that, Aspen. I was trying to make you understand the danger you were in. The danger that you're still in. Hell, the danger we're putting you in if we all make love to you and claim you as our woman for real."

"I don't care about any of that if you tell me that you really want me, and have wanted me for all this time. None of the danger, the mob stuff, matters to me. I get it. I honestly do," she told him.

Zin pulled slowly from her body and let her feet touch the floor. She gripped his arms and he could feel how unsteady she was. She was just as affected as he felt.

Storm reached out and pulled her to him by the waist of her skirt. He wrapped his arms around her and held her gaze with her head tilted back to nearly her shoulders and Storm's expression firm and serious.

"I do want you, desire you. Always have, baby, but didn't want to risk putting your life in danger. This is real, not some game to make you feel weak, vulnerable, and controllable. This is the beginning of something perfect. Something we've all wished for, wanted for too many years to think back upon. Let me show you how true, how strong my feelings for you are." Zin watched as Storm leaned down and kissed Aspen deeply, sweetly, and with such passion he couldn't help but smile.

Storm lifted Aspen up and pressed her against the wall.

"Oh my, Storm. Are you going to take me right here against the wall, too?" she asked as he kissed along her jaw and then her neck.

"Fuck no. I'm going to carry you to the bedroom, strip you of the rest of these clothes, and explore every inch of this body I've lusted for. Then you're going to let the others make love to you together. We're going to claim every hole, Aspen. All of you will belong to us completely." He gripped her cheeks and held her firmly with their gazes locked.

"No other man will ever have what's ours. Ever. Do you understand me?"

"Yes, Storm. Yes. I want all of you, too. But one thing."

He raised one eyebrow at her and the others mumbled comments about her being stubborn and recalcitrant.

"You all belong to me, too. No woman ever again but me."

Storm smiled as he kissed her lips and then carried her out of the front hallway toward the stairs and up to the bedroom.

* * * *

Storm set Aspen's feet down on the rug in the bedroom. A bedroom none of them had ever brought another woman. In fact, they'd never even had sex in this house with a woman, maybe unconsciously hoping that one day they could take Aspen here and make love to her together.

He kept his hands on her hips and slid them along to the back to undo the clasp of her skirt. He stared down into her sage-green eyes and absorbed her soft, perfect skin, lush lips, and the deep cleavage of her breasts. He knew she had an amazing fucking body. So many times over the years he'd watched her behind his dark sunglasses as she lay by the pool sunbathing at a party at friends' houses. He used to think about making love to her out in the swimming hole behind their house, a place she often swam as he pretended to be a big brother. Not any-fucking-more.

"What are you thinking about?" she asked him in that soft, calm tone that was so Aspen. He'd dreamt about her whispering things into his ear. Maybe how badly she wanted his cock in her mouth, her pussy, even her ass.

Her skirt fell to the floor and he massaged her skin, using his palms to squeeze her ass cheeks. She gripped his forearms.

"I'm thinking about you, and all the ways I've ever wanted to claim you, make love to you, and possess this sexy body."

He ran his hands along her ass cheeks, squeezed them, pulling her toward him while he explored her flesh with his hands and fingers. He ran a finger along the crack of her ass, and she gasped, her fingers digging into his skin.

"Take off your bra," he ordered her firmly, and she responded immediately. She let go of him and he continued to massage her ass, using his thigh to spread her thighs wider so he could coat his fingers with her juices.

He stroked one digit up into her pussy from behind just as she pushed the bra off her shoulders and onto the floor.

"Damn, baby, you are fucking perfect." He eyed her breasts over and saw the nipples harden before his eyes. He blew warm breath over the tiny buds and then leaned down and licked the berry.

"Storm," she whispered.

"Let down your hair. I love it down, cascading over your shoulders, framing your beautiful face, and making your gorgeous eyes stand out so bright." He nipped at her nipple using his teeth, and she moaned while she reached up and back to undo the clips holding her hair in place.

The long jet-black locks fell immediately over her skin, the scent of her perfume filling his senses, and he closed his eyes and inhaled.

"I love that smell. The scent of you. Now it's time to see if you taste as good as I think you will."

He kissed her on the mouth and then trailed those kisses along her neck, pulling his fingers from her cunt while stroking the wet digits over the crack of her ass. He let his palm slide along her hips, up her spine then to her belly as he used his mouth to explore her. His tongue licked along her breasts and played with her nipples, the mounds, and then back to her mouth again. The feel of her hands running through his hair and over his scalp were too much for him.

"Put your hands above your head, and spread your legs."

"What?" she asked.

It aroused him. Aspen didn't know how to take orders, only how to give them. It would bring him great pleasure to undo her, make her let go of the control she so desperately held on to, to maintain her emotions and get through the pain from years ago.

"Do as I say. Give me all of you, Aspen. All control, everything, and I promise I won't hurt you. You can count on me to always protect you. We all will, like always."

He looked up at her, his lips over her nipple, his cock growing harder, thicker at the sight of Aspen slowly raising her arms up and crossing them behind her head. She looked so concerned, yet turned on as her nipples hardened and her pussy leaked cream. He inhaled.

"You'll be submissive in the bedroom. At our command always. What we say, what we order, you will do with no hesitation or there'll be consequences."

"Consequences?" she asked in a whisper that had his cock throbbing hard.

He licked along her breast down her belly as he pressed a finger to her cunt.

"Consequences like a good spanking if you don't obey. Or maybe Weston and York will tie you to the bed and slap this pussy. If you're a good girl we'll play a game you really like." He slowly began to press fingers up into her pussy. "Maybe bring in Big Dave," he whispered, thrusting fingers up into her cunt as she gasped and nearly fell backward onto the bed. But Winter was there to hold her steady. He was naked and ready for them to take her next.

Her hands gripped his shoulders and she cried out her first release.

"How did you? How do you know about Big Dave?" She barely got the words out of her mouth. Storm lifted her thigh up over his shoulder and inhaled against her cunt.

"I told you I liked exploring your bedroom and getting to know everything about you, Aspen," Zin said from across the room.

Her face flushed.

"Don't be embarrassed. I for one was glad to see how long, and thick you like a cock. Although we got Big Dave beat by at least two inches all around, it let us know you can handle cocks as huge as ours," Winter told her and licked along her neck then bit gently into the muscle.

She creamed some more and Storm couldn't resist. He leaned forward, pulled fingers from her cunt, and replaced them with his tongue and mouth.

Aspen moaned louder and Storm knew he needed to make love to her. His poor dick was about to explode in his pants and that never happened before.

He pulled back and tore his clothes from his body.

"Get up on the bed. Spread your thighs, offer me that sweet, wet cunt, sugar," he ordered.

"Oh God, Storm, you're wild and bossy, even in the bedroom."

Winter moved to the side and Aspen slid onto the bed.

"You have no idea, woman," Storm told her, gripping his cock in his hand and moving toward her.

"Do as he said," Winter ordered.

Storm stepped forward as Aspen slowly widened her thighs and spread her palms up along her groin to her pussy. "Where do you want my cock, baby? Tell me."

"Everywhere," she whispered, and his heart pounded inside of his chest.

"Hmmm…we'll work on that tonight, too."

He pressed between her thighs and aligned his cock with her cunt, pushing into her in one deep stroke. At least that was his intention but then he felt how tight and how small she was in comparison to him and he slowed down.

"Fuck, you're tight."

"She sure as shit is. Fucking incredible how good it feels inside her though isn't it, Storm?" Zin asked.

Storm nodded his head and held Aspen's gaze as he eased out a little and then pushed all the way in.

She gasped and he moaned as he held himself deep within her.

Their gazes locked and she shocked him when she eased her hands back and above her head without him even telling her to do it.

He grabbed her hips and watched her large breasts bounce from his thrusts.

"Just like that. You give yourself fully to me, Aspen, as I give all of me to you, too."

Their eyes were glued on one another as Storm began a series of long, deep strokes into her pussy.

Her moans filled the room, echoed around it as the others gathered nearby. Storm tried unsuccessfully to take his time, but being inside Aspen after waiting all this time felt so good.

"I've waited too long for you, Aspen. Too fucking long."

"Storm, please let me touch you. Please?" she begged."

He lifted her hips and thrust into her again, lying over her body. He kissed her mouth, plunging his tongue inside in exploration and a quest to taste and claim every part of her.

"Touch me, baby. I'm yours," he told her, pulling from her mouth to speak against the corner of her lips.

She ran her hands through his hair as she kissed him back, lifted her hips, and counterthrust to his strokes. The pace changed from calm and slow to wild and passionate as they claimed one another.

She pressed her tongue deeper and twirled it with his, battling for control of the kiss. Somehow she tightened her cunt, her thighs causing his smooth strokes to rub deeper, tighter against her inner muscles. She was a fucking goddess and so many thoughts ran through his mind.

How many lovers had she had in her life? How many men had the pleasure of feeling this sweet, tight cunt wrap their dicks in her pleasure and claim a part of his woman?

He became possessive, determined to win over her heart, her body, and soul forever. His thrusts became harder and faster as he broke down her walls of resistance, making her limp under him and accepting to his dominance and control.

"Mine. You're mine, baby. Tell me. Fucking tell me, Aspen," he demanded of her as he pulled her thighs higher up against his waist and began a series of hard, fast, deep thrusts into her cunt.

"Storm. Yours. I'm yours, Storm." She gasped for air as she tried to say his name and speak.

"Come with me now, baby. Come now, Aspen!" he yelled.

"Storm!" she cried out, and he pounded into her so hard and fast he lost all control and came. He jerked his hips and grunted, closing his eyes and relishing in the sensations of finally claiming Aspen like he'd never claimed any woman before her.

He covered her body with his own and kissed her mouth, her cheeks, her neck, then back to her mouth again as he rolled her to the side so he wouldn't crush her.

The feel of her palms caressing his face, his neck, shoulders, and arms in such a delicate yet possessive manner heightened his emotions.

He grabbed her ass and pulled her on top of him and spread her cheeks. "We're going to claim every part of this body tonight, Aspen. Every hole, every inch will have our marks upon it. Do you understand there's no turning back now? This isn't some fling, some lust fest. This is our future. You're our future, our destiny."

Her eyes filled with tears but she didn't cry. Instead she reached up and cupped his cheek and chin with her delicate, feminine hands and she smiled.

"You're so handsome and sexy," she whispered then kissed the corner of his mouth.

He knew it was going to be a battle to gain her full trust and break down the walls she'd built around her heart. He hoped she truly knew how serious he was and that by making love and becoming their woman, that she was ultimately a target of their enemies. Things would need to change. He would need to call Nicolai first thing in the morning.

Storm hugged her to him until Winter approached and began to caress her ass and prepare her to take him next.

* * * *

Aspen knew how serious this was. She was being claimed by five made men. Men she'd lusted for and fell in love with somewhere along the way after all these years. In fact, maybe they were the reason why she failed as a lover in the past. She wasn't meant for any other men than these five.

Storm lifted her up as Winter wrapped an arm around her waist and pulled her back against his chest. He cupped her breast as York took Storm's place.

She moaned from the feel of strong, thick muscles around her. She was immediately aroused by Winter's touch and York's expression of desire. York stroked his cock as Winter placed her on top of York.

"We're going to take you one at a time the first time, but then, we're going to take you together, baby, and seal the deal." Winter suckled her neck as he pressed fingers to her cunt from behind, lubricated his fingers, then trailed one finger back against her hole and pressed through the tight rings.

Simultaneously York lifted her hips and aligned his cock with her pussy. She thrust down feeling full and naughty.

She gripped York's shoulders and he pulled her down for a kiss while he thrust up into her fully.

She moaned into his mouth and tightened up as Winter began to move his finger in her ass, stroking the area, making her feel sensations she wasn't at all familiar with.

"Move those sexy hips, baby. Absorb the feeling of being filled in two holes at once. Rock those hips and fuck York's cock while I get this ass good and ready for thick cock." Winter guided her.

"That's right, baby. Damn, your pussy is so tight and wet. I'm going to come so fast this first time," York told her as he cupped her cheeks, thrust his hips upward, and then kissed her deeply.

She wanted to please him. Had this desire to bring them such great pleasure they would never want or lust for another woman again. It became her mission to please York, to claim all of them as they were claiming her. The idea of having them fill her in every hole would be a fantasy come true. She would never be the same woman again. She would be ruined for any other man and she wondered if that were their intention.

She began to thrust her hips harder. She gripped his shoulders and stroked her pubic bone against him. Over and over again she worked her pussy over his cock and squeezed her inner muscles as York moaned and hardened within her.

"Holy shit, what is that? How the fuck?" York exclaimed as he grabbed her hips, tightened his expression, and began to thrust upward fast.

She gasped as Winter pulled his finger from her ass and York rolled her to her back and pounded into her.

"No one else ever again, Aspen. No one," he said, and she could hardly catch her breath his cock filled her so deeply. The bed shook and the headboard creaked as he claimed her fully until she lost the ability to hold on and screamed out.

"York!" she yelled, and then he thrust into her so deeply, holding himself within her cunt. She lost her breath.

"Aspen. Holy fuck, Aspen." He grunted, releasing his seed deep inside of her.

Aspen ran her fingers through York's brown hair, locked onto his hazel eyes, and felt the same emotion she saw in his eyes before she kissed him deeply.

In a flash Winter was lifting her up off of York, who moaned as their bodies separated.

"I can't hold back." Winter grunted behind her as he placed her on all fours next to York who lay there with his forearm over his eyes.

Winter wrapped his arm around her waist to cup one breast. She felt his large, hard body covering hers. "I want in. I need to claim this pussy now, baby. My dick is so fucking hard."

"Do it. Take me, Winter," she told him over her shoulder.

He wasted no time. He aligned his cock with her pussy from behind and slowly pushed into her. He cupped her breasts and thrust his hips, making himself fit into her tight channel.

When he suckled her neck, and she absorbed the feel of his thick, hard muscles surrounding her and how much she loved him, she felt her pussy cream.

"Your body knows, baby. You're meant for me, for us," he whispered and then caressed her breast and began to stroke into her deeper.

Just as he began to release her breasts, grab her hips, and thrust faster, she felt the bed dip and then the hand on her chin tilting her to the right. There was Weston, cock in hand, determination on his face while he looked her breasts over then her lips.

Behind her Winter fucked her harder and it was all so erotic. Being taken by one man after the next as his team looked on. She'd never thought of herself as a team player. More of a one-woman army ready to accomplish any project or job. But being here with them, and being claimed by the five men she loved suddenly made her feel like part of their team and ready for her new role.

Winter caressed her ass cheeks wider while he stroked into her.

Weston leaned forward and kissed her lips, claiming her mouth while she thrust her ass and hips backward.

"Fuck that's hot. Watching Winter fuck Aspen while Weston takes her mouth," Zin stated.

For the quietest one of the group, he sure was being the ringleader tonight.

Weston released her lips and gripped her hair and head.

"How about we get this mouth ready for when we all claim you together?" he asked. She knew what he wanted. She licked her lips and eyed his cock. Blow jobs never really excited her. They were more so done out of foreplay to get a guy aroused, but looking at Weston and his fine extra-large package, she was suddenly craving to taste him.

She licked her lips and Weston gripped her hair tighter, controlling her movements and leading her closer to his cock. She allowed him the control as Storm had warned her about completely submitting to them in the bedroom. It felt so good and so right, she wasn't having difficulty abiding by his rules at all.

Winter slowed his pace, allowing her time to adjust to being fucked while she sucked cock. Just thinking about doing both together made her cream some more. She wondered what it would feel like when one of them had their cock in her ass, too.

She licked Weston's cock from balls to tip.

"Easy, Aspen, nice and slow. When I come, it's going to be inside of your pussy or ass, not your mouth," he said in such a commanding tone it made her shiver.

She twirled her tongue over the mushroom top, and he pulled her deeper, obviously not wanting her to go too slow and torture him. She chuckled and then felt the finger push into her ass.

"Oh." She moaned and tightened, but then Weston pushed his cock into her mouth and she lost focus on the fact that Winter moved.

In and out both men stroked into her. She sucked and twirled her tongue, trying to concentrate on pleasing Weston while also pleasing Winter. The emotions consumed her and all she seemed to want was to please them both. She sucked and hummed against Weston's cock until Winter began to lose control and thicken inside of her. Weston pulled out and Aspen moaned her release as Winter pounded into her from behind. He pulled his finger from her ass and stroked her pussy over and over again until he came, slapping his body against hers.

She panted for breath and suddenly Winter pulled out and stumbled to the left onto the bed and Weston took his place. He grabbed her hips, aligned his cock with her wet pussy, and thrust into her to the hilt.

Aspen cried out. "Weston. Oh God, Weston." She moaned and thrust beneath him as another orgasm took control of her.

She shook and shivered as he stroked faster, deeper.

"Mine, Aspen. This body, every part of you is mine, woman." He roared his release as he thrust one last time and held himself within her.

Aspen collapsed to the bed, causing Weston to moan and pull out of her. She immediately felt the warm washcloth caressing her body as they rolled her to her back and cared for her.

"Rest, baby," Storm said and then kissed her lips. Aspen smiled contentedly, and drifted off as Storm and Winter cuddled against her.

* * * *

They didn't want to wait. They wanted to make love to her, claim every hole, and possess her so she would never think about leaving them. But they needed to take their time and not hurt her either. She was feminine and delicate. They were big men in all aspects of the words, and could hurt her. So they took turns showering and getting dressed while Storm prepared a hot bath for her and Winter held her in his arms.

"Come on, honey. Let's get you in a nice hot bath before we head downstairs for dinner," Winter told her as he rose from the bed and reached for her.

"Can't I just stay here and sleep? I'm so tired, and I don't want to move."

He chuckled. "No way. You need the bath to ease your muscles. If I'm not mistaken, you've never had sex with five men like us one after the next. We want to make sure we didn't hurt you."

She opened her eyes and held his gaze with her hand under her chin.

"What makes you so sure I've never had a ménage before?"

He raised one eyebrow at her and ran his hand along her thigh and her ass. "We know about Big Dave. Don't you think we know about your other lovers?" he said and she sat up.

"You didn't know about Jester."

He pulled her up into his arms and she cringed slightly. "Are you sore?"

"It's expected. You're all a lot bigger than Big Dave." She smirked and he chuckled.

"If you miss him, we can include him sometimes. I know I'd love to fuck you in the ass while one of the guys uses Big Dave to fuck your pussy."

She gave him a smack on his chest. "What's the point? I mean why settle for the fake stuff if I can have the real thing, and something more satisfying," she said as he carried her into the bathroom.

Storm was there waiting and testing the water. He looked her over and held her gaze. "Are you feeling okay?"

"Definitely," she replied quickly, but Storm looked like he didn't believe her.

"Okay. Nice and easy," Winter said, and he slowly set her down so she could climb into the tub.

She made a funny face as she took the first two steps, but Storm pulled her closer. He ran his hands over her back and her ass.

Her breasts were pressed up against his bare chest. "You are sore."

She cupped his cheeks and kissed him. "I'll be fine. The bath is a great idea. You guys have a whole routine, huh?" she asked, pulling from him to climb into the tub. But Storm pulled her back.

"No routine. We've never shared a woman in that bed, in this home, ever. We waited and hoped to have you, no one else, Aspen," he said firmly, and Winter was glad that he did. He felt his own temper rise at her attitude. Aspen was putting the walls back up again. She was so afraid of getting hurt and showing her vulnerability. Taking her together would hopefully break down those walls and her fears.

"Oh," was all she said as Storm lifted her up and slowly placed her into the tub.

"It's hot."

"It will be perfect. You'll get used to it and the hot water will ease your muscles."

"We'll be right back. We're taking showers and then getting dinner ready. You take your time and one of us will come get you."

She nodded her head and watched them leave.

Winter looked at Storm. "She's putting the walls back up."

"It's expected. She'll open up and let us fully inside. It will take some persuading but I think we can handle it," Storm said and smiled.

"What was that?" Winter teased.

"What?" Storm asked as they exited the bedroom.

"I think I saw you smile. I didn't think you knew how."

Storm gave Winter a stern look and Winter raised his hands up in surrender as he walked backward. "I get it. It took Aspen and that sexy body of hers to make you smile. Pretty fucking powerful."

"Go soak your head."

Winter chuckled and headed to take a quick shower.

* * * *

Aspen soaked in the tub until the water cooled. She slowly got out of the bath and grabbed a towel, pleasantly surprised to not feel any soreness at all.

She thought about what Storm said and how they never brought a woman to the house and never had sex here. She found it hard to believe, yet she did.

She went over everything that had happened today in her head. The raw emotion, the connection that became stronger as she made love to each man, and the fact that the bond that was there before that felt different. To learn that they had each lusted for her as she had for them was life altering. She'd feared their rejection and also her inadequacy when it came to sex. They'd feared placing her in danger but realized she was already in danger and really didn't care.

She had been numb to emotions, to connecting with anything living. Until them. Until tonight. She really felt like a part of them and now feared what would happen if they changed their minds and decided she wasn't the woman they wanted and desired. She also feared Andrei. How was she going to destroy him, save the guys' company, and also give the men the control they wanted? She knew they needed her submission in the bedroom, and actually she was fine with that. It aroused her, made her feel so sexy and feminine and as if she could let go and be free. But they were involved with the Russian Mafia. They would demand that respect in public, in their lives, and in this relationship.

Could she do that?

She dried off and moisturized her skin.

She looked at herself in the mirror. The love bites, the blush across her cheeks and face, and the sparkle in her eyes. She was in love with them. Had longed to be part of their team, their family, and connected to them in that deep way they were connected to one another. She almost felt it completely, yet her fears and her inability to let go when one of them wasn't inside of her seemed to linger and kill the happiness she should feel right now.

She gripped the counter and closed her eyes. Flashbacks of her abduction filled her mind.

The cage they'd chained her into because she fought every person who tried to control her and grab her. It was dirty and cold, and she sat on concrete in the darkness. She shivered as the pain she felt hit her body.

"Aspen."

She opened her eyes and gasped, stepping back, nearly losing her balance.

York pulled her into his arms and she hugged him tight.

"It's okay, baby. You're okay. You're safe here with us," he said, and she clung to him and squeezed him as tight as she could.

Then the awkwardness hit her. She was embarrassed as she pulled away slowly and wouldn't look at him.

"Let me get dressed for dinner."

He took her hand and pulled her back against him. He cupped her cheek and looked down into her eyes.

York. Brown crew-cut hair, hazel eyes, and muscles and sexiness galore.

"What were you thinking about?"

"Nothing."

"Hey, we're together now. We're one. No secrets, no walls between us."

She snorted.

"I'm serious."

She stared at him and held his gaze and knew she trusted him with all her heart. But giving into them completely and sharing her fears, the things that had kept her struggling through life and unable to sleep at night would leave her powerless and vulnerable.

"I need time, York."

He looked displeased but quickly smiled softly. "I understand. Just know that we would never hurt you or leave you. You're our woman now. Our lover, our mate, and friend, and nothing can ever come between the bond we started tonight and will continue to work on and build stronger. You remember that, baby." He ran his hand along the curves of her ass as he pulled her close and kissed her deeply.

Maybe, just maybe she could let them completely inside?

* * * *

Storm received a call from Dmitri during dinnertime. He excused himself and left the table, taking the call in the study down the hallway.

"How is Aspen?" Dmitri asked immediately.

Storm's gut tightened and he felt on the defensive immediately.

"She's perfect, why?" he asked.

"I tried calling her but she hasn't returned my calls. I was getting concerned."

"She's our concern and responsibility, not yours. Is that what this is all about?"

"You sound different, Storm. Has something changed between us? Because last I checked, you left me in charge of watching over your business interests. Considering that we're family, I would think that meant there were no issues between us.

Storm ran his hands through his hair and sighed. "Sorry, cousin."

"Not a problem. We've kept our family ties a secret most of our lives. Even though I can't see you, I can hear the concern in your voice. How are things really going with you, your team, and Aspen?"

"Things have changed, actually."

"Ahh, have you finally told her that you love her? Or perhaps she has told you?"

"What makes you think that she loves us?"

"Oh, I don't know, maybe the fact that she's risked her life to save your companies and your friend's company, too. You know you could give up your territory here in Chicago to me and concentrate on building your empire down in Texas. You've got enough friends in government and law enforcement to assist when needed."

"Since when did you become interested in security firms, dance clubs, and the nightlife of Chicago?"

"Oh, I don't know. I wouldn't mind the change of businesses. There's been some talk of Nicolai playing a bigger role out here."

"Not with Andrei taking over Sparks Industries."

"I wouldn't be so sure. He's been staying under the radar for his own reasons, but believe me when I tell you he's got things covered deep. I won't get into it now, but you have a lot of people watching your back. Say the word, and you can completely run the Texas territory and nothing else. You and the team will have your hands full. But with a woman like Aspen at your side, you'll be kicking ass and expanding even further in no time. I wish I could have landed that piece of ass."

"She's ours."

"Ahh, so you finally claimed her for real? That's good to hear. You watch her closely, though. I wouldn't trust Andrei to abide by any of the traditional rules. He's got some dirty work going on, which is also why I'm calling. Seems he's slowly moving in on your club scene. Has some dealers taking away business at the club and working in some illegal shit you guys have never allowed."

"Like what?" Storm asked Dmitri.

"Drugs, the prostitutes, and liquor scores."

"That bastard. We haven't been out of the city a full week yet," Storm replied.

"That isn't all he worked into. I went to make some final arrangements for some of our bigger deals downtown and get a call that Perkins may not be interested in dealing with us anymore. Seems someone else can get the protection he needs for a little cheaper."

"Then we need to do something about it."

"You have a choice, Storm. You can let him take this shit out from underneath you and deal with Nicolai, or you can have me handle it all for you and I'll be the one you allow to take things over."

"I need to talk with the team. This is their decision, too."

"Ultimately it's yours. You're the boss. For now anyway," Dmitri teased. Then he disconnected the call.

But it wasn't a total playing-around comment. There was truth to it and a bit of a threat. Storm had taken over the territory quickly with the help of his team and their friends. It was an area meant to be Dmitri's, but he got jammed up and wound up in the slammer for a few years. It was partially over a woman. Andrei was somehow part of it, and part of the reason Dmitri got caught and went to jail.

His cousin was seeking some of his own revenge.

Storm thought about Aspen. She wasn't out of danger with Andrei. The man would get back at her and even them. Especially when he found out Aspen was now their woman. Not that it would stop a man like Andrei from taking her. He had done it years ago to get back at Porter. Andrei should have been relieved of his duties by the higher-ups, but instead they turned their heads, feeling that Aspen wasn't important enough to protect.

Storm and his team, along with Porter and his team, felt otherwise. He would never forget that night. How drugged out she was, beaten, bloody, and about to be shipped off to some foreign country.

They risked everything to save her, and when they reached her in the nick of time, one look in her eyes, at her fragile, battered body, and he, Winter, Zin, York, and Weston vowed to protect her from danger for the rest of their lives. They'd never expected to fall in love with her. He wondered how she would feel when she found out it was them who had saved her.

* * * *

The atmosphere was filled with anticipation. Even Aspen felt on edge, needy and ready to explore making her fantasy a reality and let go completely. It made her feel antsy, a little resistant to giving so freely of herself. Yet, as she made small talk with the men after dinner and let them run their hands over her skin, lightly brush her elbow as they cleaned up together, and then kiss her gingerly, she couldn't seem to settle her nerves.

She'd made love to them already. Experienced the kinds of orgasms people dreamed about, raved about if they were lucky enough, so why, as she looked around the kitchen at these men, did she feel ready to lose her mind?

She jumped slightly, showing her anxiousness as Storm returned and placed his hands on her shoulders from behind. The men all stopped talking, ceasing to do whatever they were doing to keep busy and raise her anticipation level to a point where she would beg for their touch.

How did they do that?

Storm pulled her body back against his. She felt his hard body and even harder erection as it pressed against her ass.

His warm breath feathered over her sensitive skin by her neck and shoulder. Storm. Blond hair, dark eyes, the man was the epitome of intimidation and sex appeal. She absorbed the feel of his hands— warm, strong, powerful—as he began to massage her shoulders, causing her head to roll back against his chest.

One hand gripped her shoulder, repeatedly working the muscles and tension from the spot, while he pushed her baggy shirt away from her shoulder, exposing more flesh.

She'd fantasized about him and the others so many times. She'd wondered what it would feel like to be touched by them, held by them.

Now, here she was with Storm, a well-known made man, holding her in an instantly possessive manner. There was no denying the man's power and abilities. His strong fingers took control and possession of her much smaller, feminine frame.

He moved lower, pushing aside her lace bra with one slide of a finger, and cupped her breast. He licked her neck and tugged on her earlobe as he took from her whatever he wanted. She knew she was out of control, and instead of panicking or freaking out about needing to stay afloat, she relinquished it to Storm and took a chance on what he was giving her—the freedom to let go and just feel everything they had to offer her.

She shivered and pressed her body snugger against his front. Eyes closed, she imagined his body naked, filled with dips and ridges of pure muscle as well as old scars that she was sure he had stories for each of them. Would they ever be so close, so connected and bound that he would share those stories with her? He would want the same from her. To know the details of the one event in her life that had altered her destiny. He would want to know about her abduction and near-death experience.

She felt him pinch her nipple between his thumb and pointer. It aroused her, made her moan softly, and took her mind away from the fearful, dark thoughts of her past. She didn't want to feel that way ever again. It was her deepest weakness. If something like that ever happened to her again, she would die. Whether at the hands of strangers or by her own hands to avoid being taken against her will.

Storm applied more pressure, pulling and pinching the tiny nub until she could only focus on the sensations he was causing.

"I love the sound of your little purrs," he told her.

"Do you?" she asked.

"Oh yeah, we all do," Winter said as he approached. He reached down, grabbed her by the waistband of her light pants, and shoved them down her legs along with her panties.

She gasped.

Winter stepped in front of her and cupped her pussy as he held her gaze. "This is ours. Whenever we want it. You got that?"

She held his gaze and got lost in his powerful attitude, tone, and stance. She would do anything they asked of her. She loved them more than life itself.

She showed her acceptance to his command and claim by stepping out of her pants and widening her stance.

Winter held her gaze while he inserted a finger into her already wet cunt.

She felt it—thick, hard, and long—penetrate her vaginal muscles and get coated with her cream.

"Winter," she whispered as he began to stroke her and add a second digit. He curled his finger, added pressure on the inward motion, and hit that spot she often wondered about actually existing.

"Oh." She moaned as cream dripped from her pussy.

Dixie Lynn Dwyer

These men were amazing at seduction and control. She wanted to break that control. Penetrate it and make them feel as wild and uninhibited as they made her feel.

Storm used his hands to caress her ass. He squeezed and parted her cheeks then stroked a finger along her anus. She felt Winter remove his fingers and Storm's fingers took their place. He stroked her from behind. He sunk his fingers into her pussy, coating them with cream before he trailed his fingers back and pressed one wet digit against her puckered hole. She tightened up and he gripped her breast tighter.

"Relax and let me in. I need to get this ass ready for my cock, Aspen. You need to be slick and wet." He kissed her neck and earlobe, blowing warm breath against it, and as she relaxed a little, he inserted his finger in her ass.

Aspen moaned and Winter caught her mouth with his, plunging his tongue inside and deepening the kiss.

Behind her Storm continued to stroke her ass and she felt her pussy swell to a point where she felt so needy she wanted to cry out and demand that someone touch her there. Fuck her. Do something.

"Please," she begged as Winter pulled from her lips, his eyes carnal and dark with control.

"Winter is going to carry you out to the living room, baby. Weston's getting the lube, and Zin and York are flipping a coin to see who gets to fuck your ass while the other one fucks your pussy."

She moaned and Winter kissed her as Storm pulled his finger from her ass before Winter lifted her up and against him.

She straddled his waist, his jeans chaffing against her inner thighs as he walked her to the couch in the living room.

They were all moving about and Winter took his time holding her in his arms, caressing her back and her ass, then kissing her neck before he set her down on her feet.

Storm turned her toward him and he was now completely naked. Behind her someone pulled her shirt up over her head and then unclipped her bra and tossed it to the other couch. She looked and saw it was York. Now Winter was undressing.

Storm cupped her breasts and pulled her toward him to kiss her as he fondled the large mounds. She took the opportunity to run her hands over the dips and curves of his muscles, feeling the hard steel beneath his skin and his hips and thighs. Her hands seemed so small against his large, thick flanks. He was built like a stallion, every ounce of him pure muscle and power.

She felt aroused and brazen as she reached for his cock and stroked it.

"Oh yeah, baby, you touch me wherever you want. I'm all yours," he said and then pulled back slightly.

She lowered herself to her knees, holding his gaze as he looked down at her taking his cock between her lips.

"Hell yeah, that's hot," York said and ran his fingers through her hair and pressed her lower to take Storm deeper down her throat.

She moaned and Storm pulled from her mouth.

"Fuck, you have an amazing mouth, Aspen. We're going to put that to good use in about two minutes."

"Come here, sweetness," Winter said and she turned around to see him sitting on the edge of the couch, his cock in hand.

She wanted to suck on Storm more, and make him beg to come. But it seemed they truly liked to stay in control when it came to making love to her, so she accepted.

She crawled seductively toward Winter and could feel the hands caress over her back and ass as she approached the couch. Winter spread his thighs wider and she caressed the inner thighs until she cupped his balls.

"Come on up here and ride me."

She hesitated a moment and Storm pet her hair.

"Baby, the anticipation is killing us. We want to be inside you together. Now get on up there and ride Winter's cock so I can fuck this fine piece of ass." She swallowed hard.

But she slowly climbed up into Winter's arms and he kissed her deeply.

Storm guided her hips over Winter's cock as she gripped the muscles. She slid down over the hard, thick rod and took Winter inside.

"Oh yeah. How's that, baby?" he asked and ran his hands along her lower back then to her ass, squeezing the muscles.

It felt so good, she moaned again.

Then she felt his hands massaging her ass cheeks wider before he pressed a finger over her puckered hole. She tightened up and he held her hips.

"Easy now, baby. You ever have a dick in your ass before?" he asked.

She shook her head.

Storm gripped her hips and pressed his back against her. She could feel his cock at her lower spine.

"I'm going to be the first man to fuck this ass ever. Hot damn you know how to make a man lose his mind." He wound his hand around her hair, turning it into a makeshift ponytail close to the back of her head.

She felt cool liquid, and then hands began to massage her ass. She knew that York was joining in.

"Get that ass good and wet, York. My dick is so fucking hard," Storm said, still holding a fistful of her hair.

Storm leaned down, pulling her head back, and she complied as he kissed her hard on the mouth. In this position her breasts pushed out, and Winter thrust upward as he played with her breasts.

"She looks so perfect," Weston chimed, and she felt her pussy cream. They were all together. All watching over her, taking her as one.

Storm released her lips and York stroked fingers into her ass.

"She's ready," he said, pulling his fingers from her well-lubricated ass.

"I've been ready," Winter added, and Weston chuckled.

"Here we go, darling. Tonight we claim it all."

She felt the thick tip of Storm's cock against her anus. Winter pulled her lower and kissed her on the mouth, causing her to widen her thighs and give Storm the room to breach her ass. He pressed the thick top through her tight rings and a moment later he slipped fully inside.

"Oh!" She moaned aloud along with Winter and Storm.

Storm's grip tightened in her hair. "I'm in, Aspen. Are you okay?" he asked her.

"Yes, oh God, it burns."

"We'll ease that, baby," Winter told her and stroked his cock upward. Behind her Storm pulled slightly out and Winter thrust all the way in. They worked together, stroking and thrusting and then she felt her body tighten just as Storm released her hair and York touched her face.

"Right now, baby, this is for you, too."

He held his cock in his hand and she immediately stuck out her tongue to take a taste.

She often wondered how she would be able to take three men at once like this. Would it be awkward? Would body parts hurt and take her mind away from the deep penetration of their cocks? She got her answer as York pressed his cock between her lips and she accepted his invasion.

She sucked and bobbed her head as they worked in sync. The sensations, the fullness, and the connection were overwhelming.

"Fuck, I'm there. She's so damn tight," Winter said as he came inside of her.

Storm continued to fuck her slowly, deeply, being sure to not hurt her and she loved him for it.

York pulled from her mouth and she gasped.

"When I come, it's going to be in your ass, baby, with Weston's dick filling your pussy."

Storm wrapped an arm around her waist and hoisted her up as his strokes grew deeper and faster as Winter pulled from her body.

Weston took his place and she straddled his hips but couldn't take his dick inside of her because Storm was grunting and thrusting into her ass.

Her pussy clenched and spasmed. She felt it grow thick.

"Please. Oh God, I need more," she said.

Storm's fingers found her clit and he pulled on it, rubbing her juices around in a circular formation. She grew closer and closer to her orgasm when he pulled his fingers away, and Weston grabbed her hips, aligned his cock with her cunt, and shoved her downward.

She screamed out her release as both cocks filled her deeply.

"Oh, Aspen." Storm growled and pumped his hips then shot his seed into her ass.

Weston cupped her breasts and pulled her lower to kiss her deeply. Storm pulled from her, letting the palms of his hands caress down her back and squeeze her ass cheeks as he pulled away.

Weston then thrust upward bringing her back to the point of pleasure as another orgasm instantly started to build. She was so turned on by all of this and then felt the tip of York's cock at her anus and his one hand on her shoulder.

She widened her thighs and lifted up.

Smack.

"Oh!" she cried out, not expecting the slap to her ass.

"Fuck," York said and pushed into her ass then smacked her ass cheek again. He rubbed where he spanked her.

"Look at that nice shade of pink on her ass. I own this ass, baby. We all do. Hold on, Weston and I are going to take you for a ride." She lost her breath as both men began to fuck into her together. Weston kissed her, pulled on her tongue, and nipped her lips while York held her hips and pounded into her ass from behind her. The sounds that echoed through the room were insane.

She couldn't take much more as she lost all ability to remain upright as she screamed her release.

Weston followed, holding her against his chest as he thrust his hips and came hard. Behind her York held himself deep and roared as he shot his seed into her ass.

Their panting and ragged breaths filled the room.

"Oh God, I don't think I'll ever be able to walk again," she said and they chuckled. She instantly felt them pulling from her body, and then she felt their caresses and the warm washcloth cleaning her up. She couldn't even open her eyes. Only briefly as each of them kissed her lips and she blinked her eyes only to see who it was.

"Weston?" she whispered as he lifted her into his arms and carried her out of the living room and toward the stairs. That was the last thing she remembered before exhaustion overtook her.

* * * *

Weston felt the dampness against his chest. The mumbled whimpers and the nails that dug into his skin. It awoke him from his sleep and now Aspen was rocking against him and curling up.

"Easy, Aspen. You're okay," Storm told her as he caressed her back.

Weston cringed from the bite of her nails digging into him. "You're safe."

"York, get the light. The one on the bedside. Turn it on, hurry." Storm gave the order.

York moved quickly and the light slightly illuminated the room.

She shook her head and gasped for air. Storm spoke to her and caressed her arms. Now Winter was on the bed. York stood on the side looking over Weston's shoulder. Weston grunted at the pain her nails caused.

Storm continued to talk to her and caress her arms, bringing her back to the present.

"Easy, baby girl, we've got you. You're not there anymore. Never again, Aspen. We're here."

He kissed her damp cheeks and Weston felt her fingers ease from his skin. He held her head and caressed her hair.

"Are you okay now?" Weston asked her.

She nodded and eased back against the pillow.

No one said a word.

Weston locked gazes with Storm, the turmoil obvious on his face.

"Aspen, baby?"

"Leave the light on please. Please don't turn it off," she said and shivered as she clung to the pillow. Weston pulled the covers around her and snuggled against her back. He kissed her shoulder. "Sleep, Aspen. We've got you. You're safe."

Chapter 5

"Have you heard from her?" Nicolai asked Dmitri over the phone as he sat in the back of the limousine.

"I have. She sent me a few updates, and it's not looking good. That scumbag Andrei wants to take over more than just the clubs. He wants Pro-Tech Industries as well as Liberty Construction and Development. Those are the legit businesses Storm and his friends run," Dmitri told him.

"Most of what Storm and his team members do is legit. If Aspen is successful in weeding out the rats in the company as she seems more than capable of doing, then perhaps it's time for Storm and the men to hand over the reins to you?"

"I offered him that the other night. Seems they're making progress with Aspen."

"How does Aspen feel about that?"

"Not sure. We've limited our communication. I set her up with a clean iPad. No one can track it and she knows how to delete whatever she sends to the e-mail and burner phones we set up. It's all good."

"My concern is Andrei's interest in Aspen. If he was so pissed about Aspen securing that construction deal with Cartwright, which was incredible, then why didn't he take her out? You know, at minimum make her pay up, take some revenge on her or something. Instead he threatens her brother, Storm, Weston, and the rest of the team, including India, and forces her to work for him as his CEO? I'm sure she hasn't told Storm about any of this."

"Nicolai, she's trying to save everyone and doesn't have a care about her own life. I'm sure that stems from years ago when she was abducted and nearly sold off."

"That's the type of business our families have never gotten involved in. But Andrei has. Andrei was responsible for a lot of bad things over the years. But because of the family ties, they won't give the order to take him out. Not yet anyway."

"Well, maybe some of the newest information will help make the bosses change their minds. It seems that Aspen uncovered something else while she had me investigate some of the suspected employees of Pro-Tech."

"Like what?"

"Andrei and Demyan have been showing an interest in my charity program, Star Haven, for quite some time. Though they only recently began to show up at the yearly celebratory venues. Anyway, Storm and his team have hired many of these young people over the years for both Pro-Tech and for their clubs they own and we own."

"My clubs as well?" Nicolai asked.

"Afraid so. I have a list of individuals that could very well be sabotaging our companies. I'm gathering a team now to, let's say, interrogate them."

"I want that list. You say that Aspen uncovered this in a matter of a week working at Pro-Tech?"

"Sure as shit did. I'd snag the woman myself but she turned me down multiple times. She's an asset to the family. I mean to Storm and the team's businesses and territory."

Nicolai thought about that a moment. "Storm will need to know about this."

"He'll find out soon enough. Aspen has to keep Andrei believing that she's sabotaging the company. She said that Andrei mentioned her finding out any information on you as well. He wanted to know if you were invested in Pro-Tech and what your share was in it."

"The slimy bastard wants to rip my investments out from under me, too? He's out of his fucking mind."

"No, Nicolai, think about it. Why would he want this territory so badly? Why does he want to keep Aspen close by and unharmed? Why is he looking to land the businesses we currently have ties to even on a small scale?" Dmitri asked.

"He wants to squeeze me out. The fuck wants to be one of the heads. Son of a bitch. I think we need to keep Aspen well protected. There are other things you, Storm, and his team don't know about."

"Like what?" Dmitri asked.

"When the time comes, it will be revealed. For now get me the list. You and I will coordinate a plan with Aspen. Storm is going to be pissed that we're putting the woman him and his team love in the middle of this, but it's inevitable. When she sought her revenge against Andrei, she already placed herself in danger."

"I'll do whatever is necessary to protect her."

"Good. Keep me posted."

"You got it, Nicolai. I'll send the list immediately."

Nicolai disconnected the call and leaned back in his seat and sighed.

"Problem, Nicolai?" Karlicov, his personal security guard and closest friend, asked him.

"Seems so, Karlicov. It appears that Andrei Renoke is up to his old tricks."

"He wasn't successful years ago when he helped Iakov's brother Ivan try to take over territory that wasn't his or Renoke's."

"Yes, and he was given another chance when the true owner of that territory was revealed. But this is different. He's obviously been planning this takeover for quite some time. He's even got Sotoro involved and letting him slide into all of our businesses through the clubs. No wonder the numbers have been dropping. But he should have done his homework. He should have realized why he failed the

first time and why I took such an interest in helping Porter and Storm
and their team locate Aspen."

"Why did Andrei have his men take Aspen and try to sell her off
as some sex slave?"

"To send a message to Porter."

"But Porter was just starting out in the business. He was basically
given the territory by you."

"Andrei didn't realize that until it was too late."

"Is that why he's kept Aspen alive even though she screwed him
over? To use her again to get Porter and even Storm to cooperate?
Damn, he's a sneaky fuck. He knows that Storm and his team are in
love with Aspen."

"But what he doesn't know is that he's digging his own grave.
Aspen is more than just Porter's sister and Storm and his team's
woman. Her ties to the family run deep."

Karlicov took a deep breath and released it. "So it's true then?
What you figured out years ago?"

"Oh, it's true, and it may be the revelation that ends Andrei's life
for good. That dumb bastard will wish he never chose to fuck with my
family. He'll be begging for mercy. From the other bosses of the
family, and from me. All the shit he's pulled will finally be enough to
take him out, and with no repercussions from the other bosses."

Karlicov whistled. "Why not just make the call now?"

"And lose the opportunity to weed out any other disloyal
individuals? He'll want it this way. I'll take full responsibility. In fact,
I will make the first call. The one giving him the heads-up about
Andrei."

"What do you want me to do?"

"Put a tail on Demyan and Iakov. I want to know where they are
at all times and what their role is in all of this. They'll be going down,
too, if they choose to go against Dmitri and I. We may be getting that
blood war sooner than later after all."

* * * *

Casper's. Why is it that I love this place so much? Is it the memorabilia on the walls? All the old and new pictures of soldiers, teams of friends who served our country or gave their lives for it that make it so special?

Aspen heard some laughter and looked over her shoulder at the bar down the hallway to where Storm, Weston, York, Zin, and Winter were joking around with Gunner, Garrett, and Wes McCallister. Old friends of theirs, and of her brother Porter, too. It was out here where she recovered from her injuries after being taken.

Aspen felt her chest tighten. She closed her eyes and wished the images away. She still felt embarrassed every night when she awoke in a cold sweat, sometimes screaming for help or just begging for freedom. The men were so supportive and loving. She knew they didn't sleep well with the light always on, but they didn't complain or even leave her alone in bed at night. Instead, they all gathered around her.

She wasn't sure why she felt so safe with them. She knew she loved them and loved making love to them, but there was something else there. Some other kind of deep connection. She just couldn't figure it out, but it was there.

Aspen continued to look at the pictures on the wall when she came across one of her favorites. A picture of Weston, York, Storm, Zin, and Winter standing together in uniform all dirty and as if they'd just finished some mission. Storm didn't smile. No surprise there. It was hard to get him to smile. Winter was just as firm in his expression, but his eyes seemed to express it all. Like maybe he was relieved to be alive and to have made it to be part of the picture. Weston was smirking, leaning on some huge-ass black gun that had a telescope or something on it. In fact, she noticed they all had the weapon either on them or were leaning on it.

They were very capable soldiers. It was York who smiled the biggest, not that it was a huge smile but enough to call it a smile, not a grin. She was learning more and more about each of their personalities every day. They were different at work than they were at their home. At Pro-Tech they were serious all the time. Yet as organized, disciplinary, and hands-on as they were with the business, none of them knew or even suspected that there were spies in the company. Men and women, though she figured about six in all in this specific building, were out to help Andrei take them over.

She wasn't going to let that happen and she hoped that Dmitri could use his resources to help her, too.

Aspen ran her hand along the edge of another picture frame that contained more of a candid shot of Storm and his team when something caught her eye.

A hand gesture. Storm, dressed in black and half his face covered with something black, too, where only his eyes could be seen.

She gasped as the tears stung her eyes.

She looked toward the men standing at the bar laughing, enjoying themselves with their friends, but Storm looked at her over his mug of beer.

She turned away and headed toward the back door to get some air.

It was him. Storm was at the pier years ago when I was abducted. It was right before they were shipping her out. They drugged her because she fought the men holding her captive and they broke her arm, cut her skin, and bruised her up good. She felt the drugs taking over her body, but images flashed in her head now just like in her dreams. She heard no gunfire just gasps, then grunts and heavy things falling to the ground. She had tried to force her eyes to open when she saw shadows in the darkness then the hand gesture, like the one in the picture inside Casper's. Palm flat then raised upward then back down flat. Eyes, dark blue, widened and then appeared angry. She remembered thinking he was one of the bad guys as she tried to use her one good arm to fight him, but she was too weak and darkness overcame her.

The back door opened and she turned to look and saw Winter.

"Hey, are you okay?" he asked her and she nodded her head and turned away from him to look out at the gardens in the back of the building. On the other side was a dance floor that extended from inside to outside. The sounds of country music could be heard even out here on the other side of the building. She loved this place.

She felt the hand on her shoulder and she immediately reached up and covered it.

She wanted to cry, to just let all the emotions she felt just go. She knew the truth now. That Storm, Winter, York, Zin, and Weston were the ones to save her life when she was seventeen. Ten years ago this month. It was an anniversary she hated remembering and experiencing every year. But it always stood out in her mind.

She had so many questions yet couldn't get herself to confess that she knew the truth now. Why hadn't they told her? Was it because the doctors told them not to? They had told her to not force the memories from her mind. That when someone experienced something so traumatic in their lives they blocked it from their memory. They said sometimes things triggered the memories and sometimes the person recalled all the events they had initially blocked out.

It was this place. It was being with Winter, Storm, Zin, York, and Weston that brought back the past.

Weston wrapped his other arm around her waist and pulled her back against his front. "Are you sure that you're okay? I know we got a little wild today after work before we came here. You're not sore are you, Aspen?" he whispered his concern then kissed her neck.

She sure wasn't sore. Their lovemaking every day after work and every night before bed was heaven. Sometimes they would even take her in the morning and during the night after she awoke from her nightmares.

"I love making love to all of you. It's when I feel most complete and safe."

He kissed her neck again and held her snuggly in his arms.

"That's a good thing, baby. You are safe with us. Always," he said, and her heart filled with such deep love and emotion. They risked their lives to save her those years back. They watched over her the past few years because of Porter and their friendship. But then they fell in love with her as she fell in love with them. That was crazy.

She was going to tell him that she knew but the door opened and there was Gia.

"Aspen, there you are. Come on, girl, they're playing our song," she said, and Aspen smiled as Winter let her go.

"I'll meet you two inside," he said and winked at Aspen.

She and Gia headed back inside.

* * * *

Winter smiled as he took a deep breath and released it.

He had been watching Aspen as he, Storm, and the others reminisced with their friends. He saw her looking at the old pictures she always seemed to gravitate toward whenever she came to Casper's.

His chest tightened when he saw her staring at one picture of them in combat uniform. When Winter glanced at Storm, he had been watching Aspen, too, and they thought she'd finally figured it out. That they were the ones to save her that night from being shipped out as some sex slave. God, that fucking made him see red all over again. The broken arm, her battered skin and naked body curled up in a ball in some fucking cage like an animal.

But she didn't say a word. She didn't let on to knowing. He wanted her to know. He wanted to make her realize that they were always going to protect her and keep her safe. That they had a special connection and bond because of that situation. And now that she was part of them, part of their team, their family, they would ensure her happiness for the rest of their lives.

He headed back inside and Storm looked at him and raised one eyebrow. Winter shook his head, and disappointment filled Storm's face and then quickly disappeared. It seemed his friend was hoping for the same thing Winter was. For Aspen to know they had been the ones to save her that night, and he vowed then to always watch over her so she would never feel pain again.

* * * *

"You look a little bit out of it. What's going on? Have the guys finally made a move on you?" Gia asked.

Aspen released a sigh. "I guess you can say they did."

"Yes!" Gia exclaimed and pumped her fist in the air and then back down.

Aspen chuckled as they sat at a small high table to the corner of the room. They had danced to a few songs and were in need of something to drink.

Gia gave her a nudge. "Are you happy about it or what?"

"Are you kidding me? I've lusted over them like some teenager with a crush on the older, mysterious men. It's just surreal I guess. Being here with them. Sleeping with them," she whispered, and Gia grabbed her arm and hugged her.

"You lucky girl."

She chuckled. "They are incredible, and I've never done anything so intense before."

"Then what's the problem?" Gia pushed.

"Problem?"

"Yes, problem. You look preoccupied with something."

Aspen thought about that a few seconds. Gia was a good friend. Porter had been the one to introduce them to one another.

"You know how I described to you that feeling I had. Like there was some sort of connection between me and the guys?"

"Yes. I figured it was the attraction you felt and how destined the six of you were to be together one day."

Aspen nodded her head as she played with the glass in front of her.

"I remembered something from my abduction that I couldn't remember."

Gia placed her hand on Aspen's arm. "Oh God, what did you remember?"

"A hand signal. A disguised face with eyes I would recognize anywhere."

"I don't understand. You recognized one of the men who took you and hurt you?"

Aspen shook her head. She felt the lump in her throat as she looked at Gia. "I remember who saved me."

Gia's jaw dropped and she looked around the room and then back at Aspen, whispering. "Who was it?"

"It was them."

"Come again?"

"Storm, Winter, York, Weston, and Zin. It was them that rescued me and saved my life. I saw Storm's eyes, and then the hand signal he used, just like in one of the pictures out front."

"Are you sure? I mean that was like ten years ago, Aspen. Maybe you love them so much already and find such security and safety in their arms that you just want it to be them?"

"No, Gia. I know it was them. I feel it here." She covered her chest where her heart was. "It's what that connection has been all this time."

Gia sat back and sighed. "My God, they probably have loved you, too, for like forever."

"At night, when I'm sleeping with them, I feel so safe. I started remembering more details about my abduction. Things I thought I might never remember and that the doctors said could come back if triggered by something."

"You think the men, that hand gesture one of them did, triggered your memory?"

Aspen shrugged her shoulders. "Apparently from what I've read in the past it really doesn't take much. If you think about it, Salvation, Casper's has always been like a home to me. It's the only place I feel comfortable in."

"Don't you feel safe in their arms at night? You should now, considering you know the truth," Gia told her.

Aspen thought about that a moment. "I should be feeling safer, but I'm also wondering why they never told me. Why hadn't they made a move earlier? Are they now because I'm in a tiny bit of trouble?"

"A little bit of trouble? Girl, you fucked over a Russian mob boss making him lose millions of dollars against a competitor. I would say that you're in a little more than a tiny bit of trouble," Gia whispered, and Aspen let out a small chuckle.

"You know, now that we're talking about this. How exactly is Gunner really taking this situation? I mean, he knows or has known that Storm, Zin, York, Winter, and Weston have *connections*," she said, making the finger signal by her head to emphasize the word. "Does it cause a conflict of interest, him being a Texas Ranger and all?" Aspen asked as she often wondered how the men had friends that were involved in law enforcement and other agencies that busted people who engaged in illegal activities. Not that the men were involved in anything that could hurt someone or take their life. At least that she knew of. That made her chest tighten. As long as she had known the team, it seemed she still didn't really know who they were and what they had done in their lives.

"Gunner doesn't really say. He's not the only friend of your men that are involved in some sort of law enforcement or government agency. I think that Storm and them have helped Gunner and their other friends a few times in the past to help them solve crimes or track bad guys down. I think it all evens out or something," Gia told her, and Aspen smiled. She looked around Casper's, recognizing a few regulars and even some men and women she knew. Everything about the place, about Salvation, made sense to her. It was where she felt more like herself and able to let go. She wondered if all this crap with Andrei blew over, whether or not she should stay here in Texas. Then came thoughts of what would happen between her and the men. Could this really last forever? She wondered if they would get tired of her. Or maybe annoyed that she still had to sleep with the light on and that she still had nightmares. They were such amazing men and her feelings for them ran so deeply.

She looked up in time to see Garrett and Weston walking toward them.

"There ya are, darling," Garrett said as he leaned down and kissed Gia and then squeezed her shoulder from behind her.

"You enjoy some dancing, baby?" Weston asked Aspen as he turned her stool toward him then leaned down and kissed her on the lips.

"Yes," she whispered.

He winked. "Ready for bed? I mean to call it a night," he said and cleared his throat. Garrett and Gia chuckled.

"We'll get together this week? Maybe hit the dojo?" Gia asked Aspen as she got up with Garrett.

"Sure. Give me a call and I'll see if one of my bosses will give me some time off," Aspen teased, and Gia winked.

Weston pulled her up from the stool as Gia and Garrett walked away.

"Your bosses, huh? I think I like the sound of that. I can give you some orders and you can serve me." He leaned forward and nibbled against her neck and shoulder.

She weakened in his embrace, rolling her head to the side to give him better access to her body. He ran his hand along her ass cheek and began to rock against her with the sound of the slow music in the background.

He whispered into her air, taking her lobe between his teeth, "I want you, baby. I love that I don't have to hide my feelings for you any longer. I can touch you, kiss you, whisper my naughty, wild intentions in your ear without a care as to who's watching."

His words aroused her as well as his hands. She felt him dance her toward the side of the wall in a part of the room that was a bit darker than the rest. When he had her where he wanted her, Weston kissed her deeply.

Her back hit the wall and immediately his hand moved between them, under her skirt, and against her mound. She gasped and looked around them, pulling from his lips. There was no one watching. At least not that she could tell. But then came the thought that she really didn't care if anyone saw them. She felt possessive, and then that deep feeling of connection filled her heart.

She leaned up on her tiptoes and kissed Weston's chin and then the corner of his lips.

"I want you, too. Every day, every moment. I've lusted for you, Weston. For far too long."

She saw his eyes widen and then darken. He pressed his finger up into her cunt and she pressed her body tighter, trying to hide what he was doing from any possible prying eyes. He stroked her deeply, and she parted her lips and laid her head against his chest.

"I've lusted for you, too, baby. For many years I dreamed, fantasized about touching you, kissing you, and making you mine. I love that you're so fucking wet right now. If it were darker in here, and I was sure no one would see us, I'd lift you up, wrap your legs around my waist, and I'd shove my dick as far into you as I could get. Inside you is heaven, baby. You have no fucking idea," he told her, and she moaned as he thrust his fingers faster. Combined with his erotic words, she felt her body tighten and she gasped. He covered her mouth as she came, moaning into his mouth and rocking her hips.

He removed his fingers and caressed her back and ass then squeezed her tight.

"It's time to go home, Aspen. The others are waiting." He kissed her forehead then leaned down and grabbed her hand, taking her along with them. As they turned to leave, there stood Storm and Winter looking almost angry. Her belly tightened, and as they got closer, she saw what was really in their eyes. Hunger. Had they seen what Weston did to her against the wall? Had they watched her come, or worse, heard her moan?

As soon as she was in reach, Winter grabbed her and pulled her against his chest. He kissed her deeply until she swayed.

"Get her to the truck. We need to get home now," Storm ordered, and boy did her pussy clench with desire. They were feeling as aroused and needy as she was. Tonight, after they made love, she would tell them what she knew, and maybe even ask them why they never told her and when did they first realize they were in love with her.

* * * *

They said good-bye and then headed toward the truck. Zin grabbed Aspen's hand and brought it to his lips. He kissed her fingertips. "You are very naughty."

Weston got into the backseat of the truck as Zin lifted Aspen up and into the truck next.

Weston took the opportunity to pull her onto his lap, shoving her skirt to her hips in the process.

He gripped her skirt and her hip bones, barely feeling the thin material of her thong.

"Storm, take the long way home," he said and kissed her deeply. Aspen immediately moved her hands from Weston's shoulders to his hair and ran her fingers through it.

"Fuck that. We're taking a shortcut," Winter said, and they all chuckled.

Zin moved in next to them on the right and York on Weston's left.

The truck began to move and Weston stroked Aspen's thighs. "Lift up, darling, I need to get this pussy nice and ready for tonight," he told her, and she slowly lifted up. Weston gripped her panties and ripped them away from her body.

"Weston," she scolded, sticking her ass out behind her.

York ran his hands along her ass cheek as Zin reached over and caressed her chin.

"Don't get angry. They were in the way," Zin said.

"You're going to owe me a bunch of new pairs,"

"Why? You don't need panties around us. Ever," Weston informed her then pressed his fingers over her clit and began to massage her pussy lips in a circular motion.

Aspen moaned as Zin pulled her closer and kissed her.

Weston felt his heart begin to race a little faster. He absorbed the moment, the feel of fingering Aspen, her pussy muscles gripping his finger as she creamed more and more. He heard her moaning into Zin's mouth and could see York's hand massaging her ass cheek, maybe even playing with her ass.

The fact that Storm and Winter were in the front seat watching brought him joy as well. They had waited for this moment. In fact, they even thought it wasn't going to happen and gave up on making Aspen theirs. But no matter how hard they tried to keep her out of their head and not worry about her and want her, they just couldn't. Now here she was, kissing Zin, letting him finger her pussy while York played with her ass. It was heaven. Nothing else mattered. Not the businesses, not work, not living in the city and traveling to Chicago, to Europe, to wherever. All that mattered was being here in Salvation with Aspen and loving her.

He jerked the moment her fingers began to undo the button on his pants. She rode his finger and then pulled from Zin's mouth as she pushed back and came.

"York." She moaned and Weston lifted his ass so she could push his pants down. She gripped his cock quickly and he hissed.

"Easy, baby. Damn, your hands feel incredible."

She stroked his cock, working it between her hands as he thrust his fingers into her cunt. She moaned and began rocking her hips against his fingers then back against York's fingers.

"Our naughty little Aspen. I can't wait to get you home so I can fuck this ass with my cock instead of my fingers," York said.

"Holy fuck, she's riding both of them. Damn, Storm, get in the driveway," Winter ordered.

"I can't take it. I need you, Weston. I need both of you."

She gripped Weston's hands, pulled them from her pussy, and aligned his cock with her cunt.

Weston gave her control, leaned back, and moaned as she thrust downward on his shaft, crying out.

"Yes! Oh God, yes," she said and rocked her hips.

He grabbed her thighs and counterthrust as the truck stopped. But he couldn't focus on anything but Aspen. She pressed forward and ravaged his mouth then bit into his shoulder while thrusting on top of him. He spanned his hands over her back to her ass and squeezed her upward.

"Fuck, I can't wait," York proclaimed, and he lowered down off the seat.

The doors to the truck opened, light from the ceiling of the truck illuminating them, and Weston watched as York lowered his mouth to Aspen's ass.

She cried out and thrust backward, pushing against Weston.

"Oh God, York. Oh God, what are you doing?" she cried out and thrust then widened her thighs.

"Getting this ass wet for my cock," York said and pressed against Aspen's back.

"Widen your legs, Weston. Give me some room. I'm joining in."

"In the backseat of the truck? How the fuck are you going to fit?" Zin asked, sounding shocked. But Weston didn't really care. His own cock was so fucking hard and Aspen's pussy was milking it, working it with her inner muscles.

Weston grabbed her face and kissed her as he widened his thighs, spreading Aspen's while holding her to his chest with his cock buried deep within her cunt. He heard the creaking and moaning of the seats. Then Aspen pulled from Weston's mouth just as Weston felt York's knees hit his legs as he thrust into Aspen's ass.

"Holy shit, that is hot," Storm said, and Weston glanced to the right to see Storm leaning on the doorframe watching the scene.

To the right, Winter stood with his arm on the doorframe appearing pleasantly surprised. It was all so erotic and natural for them to be watching one another and taking Aspen like this.

He wasn't exactly comfortable, but his cock felt about ready to burst with every stroke from York.

"I can't take it. I'm going to come," Aspen said.

The sound of the truck rocking and moaning from their thrusts fed their egos. It was like something out of a teenager's wet dream to fuck a girl in the backseat of a vehicle, making the entire vehicle rock. Here he was, nearly forty, and he was finally having a youthful fantasy come true with the woman of his dreams and his team, his best friends and family, watching and participating.

It made him wild with lust and desire as he began to move faster with York as Aspen rocked in between them. Her pussy was so wet and slick he felt it everywhere.

Weston used some inner thigh and hip muscles he never knew he had to counterthrust against Aspen and York. It only took about three strokes when he felt his cock explode and come.

"Holy shit!" he cried out.

"Oh!" Aspen screamed until her voice was horse as she came. York followed, pumping his hips so hard and fast that the truck continued to rock and shake.

"We're going to need new fucking shocks," Zin teased.

The three of them panted and York kissed Aspen's shoulder then pulled from her ass.

"Oh God, York," she whispered.

He caressed her hair and Weston hugged Aspen to him. "You definitely can fill every fantasy a guy has ever had," he told her then kissed her.

"Well now it's time she fills ours," Storm said and reached for her.

Weston released her to Storm. His cock ached as he pulled from her pussy. But he caressed her ass under her skirt that fell into place as Storm lifted her up and out of the truck.

"That was so fucking incredible," York stated as he zipped up his pants.

"How the hell did you think of that, never mind actually fit in that space to do that?" Weston asked.

York ran his hands through his brown hair. His hazel eyes sparkled and he smiled. "Aspen does it to me. I love her, Weston. I love her more than anything in this world."

Weston smiled. "Well hell, York, join the fucking club. I love her, too."

York chuckled and they took their time getting out of the truck knowing that now Aspen was with Storm, Winter, and Zin.

* * * *

Zin undressed and then helped Storm and Winter take off Aspen's clothes. Winter looked for the lube as Zin pulled Aspen forward and suckled her breasts. She held his head and ran her delicate fingers through his hair.

"I love your breasts, baby. Every time we saw you out in one of your fancy gowns or at a glamorous event it drove me wild. Knowing that I couldn't touch you. That I couldn't cup your breast like this and take a taste." He cupped her breasts, squeezed the mound, and then licked the tip.

"Oh, Zin, I wish you would have made a move," she told him as she softly ran her fingers through his hair.

He suckled harder, knowing how difficult it had been to ignore the desire.

She pushed him backward and onto the bed, causing him to release her breast.

She straddled him and took his cock in her hand and aligned it with her cunt.

They locked gazes as she used her one hand to press above his shoulder on the bed so she could maneuver onto his shaft.

She held his gaze as she sunk onto his cock.

"I love when you're inside of me. It's when I feel safe and alive," she whispered then hugged him tight.

Zin held himself within her, running his hands along her back and her ass, squeezing and thrusting upward.

"You feel like heaven, baby."

She licked his neck and then jerked, and he knew the others were joining them.

He couldn't believe how turned on he was by sharing Aspen with the team. They had been through everything together and would be like this forever. One team, one family.

"I think my baby wants a cock in her ass, Storm," Zin said as he caressed her ass cheeks wider.

"I think she wants two more cocks inside of her," Winter said as he climbed onto the bed with his cock in his hand.

"I think the three of you are pretty damn smart," Aspen teased. Storm chuckled but Zin thrust upward, making her fall forward.

"I got something right here for that sexy little wiseass mouth," Winter informed her, and Aspen turned toward Winter's cock and smiled.

She swallowed, too, as Winter caressed her hair and moved her closer to his cock. Zin watched her take Winter's cock into her mouth and Winter moaned.

"Goddamn, I love this mouth."

"Goddamn, I love this ass," Storm said, and Aspen tightened up as Storm lubricated her ass then thrust his cock into her.

A series of moans went through them, and then they began to move. Zin thrust in and then out. Storm thrust next as Aspen rocked into both of them while sucking Winter's cock. They continued to move like this, finding their sync until all that could be heard was moaning and bodies slapping together.

The bed rocked and creaked.

Storm grunted and moaned. "Oh hell, my dick is so hard. Fuck, baby, I love this ass. I love it," Storm said.

Smack.

"Fuck!" Zin yelled as he felt Aspen cream, causing him to come inside of her. He jerked his hips, wanting to continue but knowing he was already long gone.

"Grrr." Winter growled and came in Aspen's mouth. She swallowed and suckled him until Winter was begging for mercy.

Storm continued to thrust into Aspen's ass, smacking her ass cheeks in between thrusts until she screamed her release and pushed back against Storm. It earned her a series of slaps to her ass and then Storm wrapped an arm around her waist and thrust into her ass three hard fast strokes before he came.

Aspen fell to Zin's chest and he hugged her to him as Storm pulled from her ass and went to retrieve a washcloth.

They took care of Aspen and Zin held her in his arms until he heard her calm breathing and knew she was asleep.

"I love you, Aspen," he whispered before he closed his eyes and smiled contently.

Chapter 6

Aspen felt her body jerk backward as she left the small business office she was working for after school. Then came the cloth over her mouth and the feel of her falling backward as her heel broke on the ground. She tried to scream but his hold was strong as she struggled to get free from her attacker. Then she saw nothing. She felt nothing until the cold, damp sensation pressed against her naked skin. A rancid smell filled her nostrils and she moaned in pain.

Blinking her eyes open she felt the heaviness against either side of her. She looked. Who were these women? Why were they all huddling together? Some were crying, whimpering in fear and pain, while others lay bloody and motionless. It hit her all at once. The realization that she was no longer in Texas, no longer on her way home to her small apartment, but instead a victim of abduction.

She tried to move her body and dislodge the weight of all the other women lying on top of one another like some shield or something. "Don't move. They'll hit you again and drug you up," one young woman whispered. Her eyes were swollen shut, her lip torn and her blouse ripped nearly all the way off.

Aspen shivered as she realized she was only wearing her bra and panties, and looked and felt pretty battered herself.

"Where are we?"

"I don't know. It's too dark in here," she whispered.

They heard male voices, the sounds not so foreign to her. *Russian? Slavic? Romanian?*

She moved into a sitting position and the young woman next to her grabbed her wrist. Aspen gasped at the pain. She wondered if her wrist was sprained or broken.

"Who's talking?" The voice came from behind them. Deep, thick accent and all. The woman screamed as the man pulled her up from the pile, stepping over bodies in the process.

He smacked her across the mouth. The woman cried out.

"No! Stop that. Don't hurt her. What are you doing? Let me go!" Aspen screamed out as she jumped up and attacked the man hurting the young woman.

His arm moved so quickly, the grunt and the gurgling sound indicating what he had done.

Aspen stepped back, falling over the other women who now cried and moaned, pleading for life.

The woman fell from his arms, all bloody. Dead. He'd stabbed her.

Aspen ran. Her legs ached. She damned not being able to run faster, because of the pain and the bruises covering her body. She could hardly see but there was a dim light. It was a good distance away, but the fear, the need to live and get free, was greater than the pain.

She felt the blow to the back of her head then the pain as her knees hit the concrete. She fell forward, the man landing on top of her. He was yelling in Russian and she was fighting him off. She swung her arms, her legs. She even bit him, and then he snapped her arm, breaking the bone. She screamed but continued to fight him until some other men came, grabbing at her, holding her down. His face was inches from hers.

"You go first, cunt. The boat leaves in an hour," he spat at her. Then she felt the prick to her skin.

She cried and pleaded to be free, to be let go and to get to Porter. Her mind went fuzzy and she fought to hold on as they threw her into a metal cage, pulled her broken arm forward and attached handcuffs to it and then the top of the cage. The pain was excruciating as her broken arm hung from the top of the cage on the inside. She barely fit into the thing. He shoved her in there, said filthy disgusting things to her as he cupped her breasts, pinched them, and laughed, telling the men he might fuck her before she was shipped off.

She cried out, screamed at him, and he slugged her in the mouth, ripped her bra off, and grazed her with the knife he had killed the other woman with. "Keep your mouth shut. I'll be back for you so we can play in just a few minutes."

She shivered and shook with fear. She fell backward and felt as if her arm would tear in half. She blinked in and out of consciousness fighting to hold on in desperation yet wondering if she should succumb to the sedative and give in to unconsciousness so she wouldn't feel the man's hands on her when he raped her.

She moaned and grunted. "Stay awake, stay awake," she chanted out loud. Then she felt the second prick to her skin.

"She's a tough bitch. Will make a great fucking slave won't she?" one man said.

"She sure will. I'd love to have her for my own. But taking her means so much more," the other said in a thick Russian accent. She recognized the voice and fought to hold on to her mind and figure out who it was. Time passed, the pain intensified to a throbbing, painful ache where she began to wish she would just die.

Her head rolled back. She felt the room spinning, the sounds seeming to echo in her mind as if they were miles away instead of very nearby. She heard thumps, yelling, then silence. Such an eerie silence.

The cage moved. She blinked her eyes open and saw the mask. It was black, covering only the man's mouth and something was over his head, too. It was as if he were wearing scuba gear but not rubber. His eyes. She focused on his eyes as she moaned. Dark blue, angry, determined, then calm. He lifted his hand and gave a signal. She felt motion around her, the click of the handcuffs dislodging from the metal above, and then her arm fell. It was numb. She couldn't feel it.

There were mumbled words. Words she didn't understand as she forced her eyes to remain open. Dark blue eyes held her gaze, transfixed on her trying to infuse strength in her somehow.

"Storm?"

"Yes, baby. Come on now. Wake up and look at me, baby," he whispered and she felt his hands on her touching her, caressing her.

Then came the Russian voice. "You both die."

The gunshot echoed in her mind as she watched Storm get shot and fall to the ground dead. The Russian. The one who'd said he wanted her for his own showed his face. "Iakov," Aspen screamed in terror and fear. Storm was dead. Storm had been shot. Storm, Storm, Storm!

Aspen was screaming over and over again as she awoke, sitting upward and rocking back and forth.

Storm was right next to her and so were Winter, York, Zin, and Weston.

She locked gazes with Storm's concerned eyes and threw herself into his arms and hugged him tight. She cried hysterically like she hadn't done in years. Not since she had been held against her will.

"It's okay now, baby. I've got you. You're safe now. It was just a bad dream." Storm's strong voice rumbled through his chest and against hers. She squeezed him so tight as it all came back to her. The memories of her abduction, the pain of her bruised and broken arm. It was so wild. Even now, her arm ached as if remembering the pain.

She felt the hands caressing her back, her thighs, and with the room illuminated, she began to settle down, remembering where she was and how safe she was.

She pulled back and Storm cupped her cheek, the look of concern and sadness filling his eyes.

"I love you, Storm. I love every single one of you guys. I've loved you forever. Do you know that? Do you know how long I've loved you? I don't care how long you've wanted to have sex with me and kiss me and hold me in your arms. Just know I love you and I figured out why the five of you have always been so important to me. Why I felt this deep connection to each of you," she said as tears rolled down her cheeks and she reached out and caressed Winter's cheek then ran her hand along Zin's arm before taking Weston's hand and squeezing it. York caressed her thigh and she nodded at him and then looked at Storm.

"We love you, too, baby. It's more than just sex, than just wanting to hold you, kiss you, and have you in our bed," Storm told her.

She cupped his cheek. "I know everything now."

"Do you know how long we've loved you?" Zin asked her.

She shook her head. "You saved me. All of you. I don't know how you did it. I don't know how you found me there, dying, giving up hope that I would make it out alive before they shipped me out."

"Don't. Don't talk about it," Winter said and cupped her cheek, running his finger along her chin and jaw.

She shook her head and smiled. She reached up and kissed his lips then pulled back. She looked at Storm, took his hand, and placed the palm over her heart and held it there.

"I remember. I saw your eyes, Storm. I saw the mask, the anger, the determination, and the fear in your bold blue eyes as you unlocked the cage I was in and saved me. I thought you were shot in my dreams. That's why I screamed your name. But it was my own fear thinking that I could lose you now that I know the truth about what you all did to rescue me. You all saved me back then. Ten years ago. Ten," she said in disbelief.

"We got the call from Porter that you were abducted. He was freaking out, and had no way of finding you. We had to use our resources, and when we did and found out their intentions…" Zin stopped talking. Storm took her hand and brought it to his lips. He kissed the top of her fingertips and ran his hand down her arm gently, repeatedly.

"You were so bruised up and battered. Your arm. God, baby, your arm looked mangled."

"You saved me."

"We've loved you a pretty damn long time, Aspen. Maybe loved you from that moment we saved you, but in more of a protective way. Like you were bound to us and us to you because we shared that experience together. It was always there. This connection," Storm whispered.

She nodded her head. "I know, Storm. I felt it, too. I just didn't know why I felt that way about the five of you. I thought it was some schoolgirl crush. My brother's older, mature male friends, so sexy and muscular. Throw in being made men and what's a young, horny girl to feel?" she said teasingly.

They chuckled. Weston wrapped an arm around her waist and squeezed her to him. "Horny, huh?" he asked.

She chuckled.

She looked at Storm, Zin, and York then Winter. "Why didn't you tell me?" she asked them.

Weston released her and she turned around, kneeling on the bed to face them as they gathered around her there.

"The doctor said to let you remember on your own and to not push it," Zin told her."

"Well that, and we basically committed about a dozen different crimes to get to you, to locate you, rescue you, get you out of there, and get you medical treatment," Winter informed her, and they laughed as they mumbled some comments about the scary experience.

"Holy shit, I remember thinking that Storm was going to get us all kicked out of that hospital in Monterrey for being right on top of the doctors treating you," Weston said.

"Monterrey? Mexico?" she asked.

"Hell yeah. Those fuckers were going to ship you out within the next few minutes and we got to them, took them out, then got to you right before they were moving your cage," York told her.

"I heard thumps and groans," she said.

"We had to eliminate a few assholes before we lost the opportunity to save you quietly. After all, we were basically in a foreign country without permission," Winter said.

"Not that we never did any such things like that before while serving our country," York teased and they chuckled.

"Fucking-A!" Weston cheered and they all laughed and hooted.

Storm cupped her cheek and brushed his thumb over her bottom lip. "We're never going to let you go, baby. We love you. You're our everything."

"And I love you, too. All of you." She hugged Storm tightly and he maneuvered her to the bed as she held him and kissed his neck. Weston moved in behind her as York, Zin, and Winter gathered around all of them on the bed.

She closed her eyes and relished in the moment of happiness. Eyes closed, breathing natural and calm, she thought about how perfect this was and how there was no other place she would rather be. Then she heard the voice in her head. The sound of the man who was giving the order to ship her out to be a sex slave and how she would make a good one.

Iakov. You slimy fucking bastard.

Did Andrei know? Andrei said that it had been a mistake. That she wasn't supposed to be taken and sold, that she was supposed to be his. He said one of his men screwed up. Did he mean Iakov? It couldn't be. Something wasn't right. Why did Iakov try to get rid of her? He was a main guard to Andrei, too.

She would need to talk with Dmitri right away. Something was going on here. Andrei wanted to own her, possess her, yet he allowed her to come here and work Pro-Tech from the inside. Now either he was a pompous asshole who thought his threats and his position in the Russian mob so great that she would obey him, or he'd set her up. Maybe even counted on her falling in love with these men so he could hurt all of them. Maybe get rid of all of them.

She needed to clarify that list of names and find out who the rats were pronto. Andrei and Iakov were going down for good. No one was going to mess with her men, her family, ever again. No one.

* * * *

When Porter arrived at the house on Sunday, he could tell that things were different. His friends, his family as far as he was concerned, had finally made their move and claimed his sister Aspen as their woman.

He thought he felt a bit of nervousness. Perhaps it was that brotherly protectiveness he always had when it came to Aspen, but it quickly disappeared as she smiled wide, Storm's hand protectively and possessively at her waist with the others surrounding her.

"Porter!" she exclaimed and ran to him. Her long onyx hair cascaded down her back and bounced as she closed the space between them. She looked so mature, sophisticated, and gorgeous one second, and then so youthful, energetic, and like a child who'd received the present she had been asking for at Christmas.

He lifted her in his arms, twirling her around like he always did, and hugged her tight. He kissed the top of her head and she squeezed him snuggly.

"I missed you, bro," she said. Feeling her in his arms, safe and secure in one piece gave him hope that she would be just fine. "I missed you, too, sis. God, I was so worried about you. About all this shit with Andrei Renoke."

"I know. It will be okay, Porter," she said, looking up into his eyes. He smiled and held her by his side until his own team members cleared their throats.

"Aspen, hot damn, girl, you look amazing," Piers said as he pulled her into his arms and kissed her cheek then hugged her. Porter shook Storm's hand and then Winter's as the rest of his own men, Ren,

Reid, and Silas took turns hugging Aspen hello and then joining in shaking everyone else's hands.

"So ya really got yourself into something good this time, huh, Aspen," Silas said, wrapping an arm around her shoulder and walking her away from everyone.

"Nothing too bad, Silas," she replied.

"My sister India says otherwise," he replied and continued to walk away with Aspen.

"So, how was your flight? Did you get in last night on time?" Winter asked Porter.

"Sure did. Got a good night's sleep," Ren said and then walked over toward York.

"What are you making for lunch and dinner?" he asked and York chuckled.

"You mean what are *we* making for lunch and dinner. Come on, let's grab some beers for everyone and go out on the back porch," York suggested. Porter watched Piers and Ren walk out of the room along with York and Zin. Winter, Weston, and Storm remained behind with Porter and Reid.

"Any new updates yet?" Porter asked Storm.

"Nothing but chatter. Got news that Andrei is still pushing into the family territory. We've got men on Sotoro and hoping to get some info to use against Andrei," Winter said.

"Aren't you guys worried about him taking over your territory and gaining more power?" Reid asked them.

Storm looked at Winter and Weston. He crossed his arms and kept a firm expression. "To be honest, Porter, we really don't care. We love your sister, she loves us, and we're together. Our fear in pursuing her has always been that threat to her life. With our connections, our positions in the Russian Mafia, and ties to Chicago, we think it wouldn't be such a financial loss, or power loss, losing the businesses in Chicago and moving out here completely," Storm told him.

"Are you serious?" Porter asked. "You'd give all that up for my sister and face the family and their lashing out? Because you know the bosses are going to flip."

"I didn't say that I was going to give it up to Andrei. I'm thinking of passing it along to someone close to me. Someone who already is there, has a good business sense, and of course the reputation of power even greater than ours."

"Holy shit, Dmitri?" Reid asked.

Winter nodded.

Porter whistled and looked toward the living room where Silas was with Aspen talking.

"What about Aspen? How does she feel about moving out here completely?" Porter asked.

"We haven't discussed it entirely yet. There's all this shit to figure out and handle about Andrei. The bosses aren't looking like they're ready to eliminate him quite yet even after all he's done in the past. Getting Aspen here and offering her the job retraining our staff and becoming part of Pro-Tech will help her become comfortable here. At least that's what we're hoping for."

"She needs to remain under your protection constantly, Storm. Renoke cannot get his hands on my sister."

"I know that. She is under our constant protection and will never be left alone."

Porter felt his anxiety rise. "Silas is worried about his sister. We think it may be a good idea to get India out of Chicago, too. We're thinking about sending her into another town with some of our friends from the SEALs."

"Who?" Weston asked.

"Flynn, Ford, Fenton, Fisher, and Gray. Gray's a deputy with the Town of Pearl Sheriff's Department. The others do protective details like this for good friends. Silas trusts Gray, and Fisher is a Texas Ranger. Pearl is a pretty unique town and with all the retired military around it would be a safe place to put her," Reid stated.

"There's also the women's shelter there. Blade, Beau, Avery, Asher, and Cason could set things up with the sheriff and the women who run the shelter to hide India there for as long as needed. Then Gray and his team could watch over her from afar. Knowing India, she isn't going to take something like this lying down. She'll fight Silas tooth and nail," Winter told him.

"I know. Silas knows that, too, but he'll personally deliver her to Pearl and make sure she understands the seriousness of the situation," Porter replied and they chuckled.

"Good luck with that. Have you seen India in action lately? It's going to take a hell of a lot to slow her down and keep her under wraps. The woman is a spitfire," Weston said and they chuckled.

"Let's grab some beers with the guys and sit out back," Winter suggested.

"I'm going to check on Silas and Aspen," Storm said.

"No need, commander, I've got her right here. We were just catching up," Silas said with his arm wrapped around her shoulders.

"Well, maybe you can catch up without touching her. I know I'd feel a lot better," Storm said, and Silas removed his arm and saluted Storm. They laughed and Storm immediately pulled Aspen against him and kissed her.

"There are consequences for flirting with other men," he teased.

"Other men? You mean Silas and the gang. That's funny, Storm. They're like brothers to me," Aspen stated.

"That's interesting, I thought you referred to Storm, Winter, Weston, York, and Zin as brothers to you, too, in the past," Silas said, and they all started laughing, but Aspen gave Silas's arm a smack.

"Don't go causing any trouble, you," she said as they started heading into the kitchen. Porter took his sister's hand and Storm stopped then winked at Aspen before he released her to her brother.

Porter knew that Storm and his team would protect her, just like always.

* * * *

Aspen took Porter's hand and they headed out to the front porch.

They were a few years apart. He helped raise Aspen when she was little and their dad was sick all the time. They'd lost their mom when Aspen was only a few months old, and their father died when Aspen was three. She didn't even remember him. It weighed a toll on the family from what Porter had told her. They had extended family that helped out for years. It made her feel more like and orphan than someone who had parents but died before she even got to know them.

"How are you really doing?" Porter asked her as they sat down on the bench.

"I'm hanging in there."

He smiled. "So the guys finally made a move on you. I thought it would never happen. But I guess seeing your life in danger again kind of changed things for them."

"Again?" she asked.

"Aspen, when you were abducted."

"Porter, I know. I know that it was Storm, Winter, Zin, York, and Weston who rescued me."

"You do? When did you know? Did they tell you?"

She shook her head and wound her fingers together on her lap. "I still have nightmares, Porter. I sleep with the lights on every night."

"What? Why didn't you tell me? We could have spoken to the doctors and gotten you something to help."

"No, Porter, I didn't want to depend upon sleeping aids or something I could become addicted to. Every night I would remember a little more. But when I came here, when I was back in Salvation, things changed for me."

"Changed how so?"

"I feel like this is home. I don't know. I mean I never really felt right at the place we had in Chicago. Every time you brought me here after the abduction and every time I visited and even worked temporary jobs around here, I felt like I belonged."

"I get it. I feel that way around here, around Tranquility and even in Pearl where I visited. The towns aren't that much different."

"I don't think I ever really felt like I belonged, Porter. I never knew our parents."

"I never really knew them either, Aspen. Then when Mom died, there were people always around taking care of us, but there were so many different faces."

"I remember that, too. I know it was part of the reason why you left and joined the service."

"I made sure that you felt strong enough to handle things, and you seemed so strong."

"I am strong. A lot stronger than you give me credit for."

"I think you're strong," Porter told her.

"Then why didn't you tell me that it was Andrei who was responsible for my abduction?"

"Because I knew you would do exactly what you did. Seek revenge. There's always been this side of you, Aspen, so tough and ready to fight and take on the world. You never back down. No obstacle is too big. It's why you succeeded in life and keep succeeding. You have a gift. Even Aunt Oxsanna saw that in you immediately. She always said how strong, how brave and determined you were, even as a baby."

"I miss her. She was a wonderful woman. To lose her to that car accident was so upsetting. I think that's when I really started to build a wall around my heart."

"Then you were abducted."

"I still don't get why. I mean Andrei told me it wasn't supposed to happen like that. I was to be his, not sold off as a sex slave."

"When did he say that?" Porter asked, and the door to the front porch pushed open.

"Did I hear you correctly?" York asked.

Aspen sighed. "He was trying to get under my skin. He was being pompous when he told me that," she said and thought about that moment and how angry she was. But then she remembered him saying how one of his guards, his men, made a mistake and that she wasn't supposed to be sold. Did he really know that Iakov was the one to take her? Or was he trying to cover something up? Was it part of a plan? But why? She knew no one in the Mafia. She was seventeen years old and working at a small business office in town when she was taken. It didn't make any sense.

York stood next to her as Porter took her hand. "That fucker told you that?" Porter asked.

York caressed her hair from her cheek and she glanced up toward him. She could see the concern and anger in his hazel eyes.

"It's not a big deal. He expected to shock me or maybe test me."

"Why didn't you tell us?" York asked her.

"He had a lot of things to say."

"At the party that night on the balcony or the day you ditched the guards we placed on you and you disappeared for two hours?"

"Aspen, were you with Andrei that night? The night they were looking for you and the guards lost you?" Porter asked.

"I had to go. Iakov and his friends were at the restaurant where India and I were having lunch. Iakov said that it would be in my best interest to make sure that I lose the guards and meet him at his restaurant."

"And you went?" York asked, pulling back and running his fingers through his hair. He was pissed off. So was her brother.

"Why would you do that? Why, after what he told you he did to you?" Porter asked.

"Because he threatened your lives and India's. I wasn't going to get you all hurt or killed. I'll still do whatever is necessary to protect the people I love," she said and stood up.

Porter grabbed her arm. "Goddamn it, Aspen, these are killers. Men who would think nothing of hurting you, raping you, fucking killing you. I can't lose you, Aspen. You're the only family I have left."

"You're not going to lose me. I knew what I was doing. I had no choice when he threatened you and India. She was with me at the restaurant. If they were able to locate us and had the nerve to approach us with Storm's security guards there, then they would come through on their threats of hurting her or you. I had to go."

"Fuck!" York exclaimed.

Porter placed his hands on her shoulders. "What happened at the meeting with Andrei?"

She didn't say a word. She wasn't sure how to approach this without blowing everything her and Dmitri were working on. But she'd never lied to Porter before. She also was a different person than she was a few weeks ago. She was in love and five men had broken down the walls around her heart and made her feel again. When she dealt with Andrei back in Chicago, she was hollow inside and didn't care if she lived or died. Now things were different.

"Aspen?" York pushed.

"I can't say."

"What?" Porter yelled out.

"I'm sorry but none of what he said matters."

* * * *

Iakov watched as India walked out of the building and headed down the street. He had two men on her as he watched them heading toward him. He'd gotten the order from Andrei to send a message to Aspen that he meant business and that she was working for him, not Storm and the others. Iakov would have never let Aspen leave. To this day he still wondered how they found her in that Mexican hellhole. He had covered their tracks so good. Why had Andrei called off selling her? She was a nobody. A woman who came from shit. She didn't even have any parents and lived with relatives. Her extended family were peasants, nobodies who worked blue-collar jobs and struggled to make ends meet. Why had she been so important to keep? Because of her beauty and sexy body?

He wanted to fuck her and then ship her off. No one would have known a thing. She was ripe for the taking. He'd issued the order, got out of the place, and then got the call ten minutes later that they had been invaded by soldiers dressed in black.

He should have known it wasn't a federal military operation. Then came the additional order to keep her alive and to stay clear. Something happened to make Andrei pull back and remain away for all these years.

His boss was weak. Iakov knew that. He didn't have it in him to slit a throat here and there to send a message. No, he wanted things operated in a more diplomatic, calm fashion. But that was what destroyed empires. Iakov could do a better job of leading and working the black market businesses than Andrei Renoke. Instead he was Andrei's main guard. Well, he gave him the job of sending a message to Aspen about loyalty to her boss, the man that now owned her as far as Andrei was concerned.

He would send a clear message. No other bitch was safe. Aspen's brother and team weren't either and definitely not Storm and those other Russian weaklings.

He made eye contact with his men and they grabbed India just as she waved down a cab. The black van pulled up. The two men took her into the van and they took off before anyone even noticed a thing.

* * * *

India was screaming and kicking her legs as the hand covered her mouth and men pulled her into a van. The sound of tires peeling out and down the street echoed in the background. She was scared, shaking with fear.

"Cooperate," one man said in a Russian accent.

The van swerved, the engine roared, and she knew they were taking her away from the city or maybe just somewhere no one could hear her pleas for help.

Then suddenly the van stopped.

One man held her hands behind her back, and made her kneel upward in the van. The door slid open and there was Iakov, the man from the restaurant she and Aspen had lunch at that day. He was Andrei Renoke's main guard.

He was an evil-looking dick who eyed her over in a way that warned any woman with a brain that the man was sleazy.

"What do you want from me?" she asked him.

"To give Aspen a message from Andrei. Remind her who she is working for." He struck her across the face once, twice, then a third time as she cried and fell over. The others joined in punching her, ripping her dress, then touching her breasts and her intimate parts. She screamed and tried to fight them off and defend herself against their hits. She felt her eye swell up, her lip, too, and she was bleeding, aching everywhere when finally Iakov gave the order to stop.

He gripped her face. She cried out.

"You tell that little bitch remember who she works for now. Andrei will not allow his woman to fuck him over again. Next time she dies."

She looked up at him and spat blood at his face.

One of the men gripped her tighter.

Iakov wiped her bloody spit from his face and gave the guy holding her a nod.

He tilted her chin up and Iakov smiled.

"Some women never learn when to keep their mouths shut."

He struck her one last time, sending her to the floor of the van.

* * * *

Storm came to the porch door with his cell phone in his hand.

Aspen turned to look at him as he stared at her.

"I just got a call. India is in the hospital. Andrei's men got to her."

"No! No!" Aspen screamed out. "Is she okay? What did they do to her?"

"They beat her up. Dmitri is with her now. He said he needs to talk to you, Aspen," Storm said and handed her the cell phone.

All eyes were upon her as Silas and all the other men came outside.

"Dmitri?" Aspen whispered, her voice cracking.

"He was sending a message. You're to remember who you work for. Remember that you're his woman and you won't get away with fucking with him again."

"Oh God, is India okay, though. They didn't..."

"No. No Aspen, they roughed her up good and she's so scared. I know that Silas wants to head out here, but I think you guys are going to need the backup there. I already spoke with him. They'll get her to a safe place. Until this all blows over, we need to keep her out of harm's way now. The fight is on Aspen."

"I want to see her. I should fly out and—"

A series of "No!" went through the porch and over the phone.

"I'm sending you everything I have. Tell the men what you've been doing at Pro-Tech. Tell them about Sparks Industries and how you stopped the sale to Andrei."

"What?"

"You were right. Gary Sparks couldn't be forced to sell the company to Renoke. It appears that he shared the company with a few silent partners."

"A few? Who?"

"I don't know, but it just put a halt to Renoke's ability to overthrow your men's territory. The individuals who owned part of the shares just bought out the company, including Gary's shares, and now there is one sole owner."

"Who?"

"No one knows."

"But then Sparks Industries doesn't stay in Storm's family. So we lost it anyway," she said to Dmitri.

"What's going on?" Storm asked, and the others looked concerned and angry.

"My sources say it does. When I know who specifically, we'll talk and I will let you know. In the meantime, you need to help Storm and the team clean house at their company. I'll send everything to them now."

Aspen ended the call and handed it to Storm, who eyed her suspiciously. She felt intimidated by him and his superiority.

"Okay, Silas is working on getting India to a safe location while we save your company, guys," Aspen told Storm, Weston, York, Zin, and Winter.

"Dmitri said that Iakov told India to tell you to remember who you work for. To remember whose woman you are," Storm announced.

"Yeah well, about that."

"Aspen," Porter said her name through clenched teeth.

"The man's delusional," she retorted.

"Aspen." Storm raised his voice.

"Okay fine, about that meeting I had when I ditched your two security guards. Well, during that meeting I found out that my sort of boss, Gary Sparks, was being forced to sell his company to Andrei, not you guys, even though I had Gary ready to call you and make a deal. That kind of went amuck because apparently, due to your whole Mafia territory thing, Andrei wants to take you over. He was already moving in on your territory at the clubs, the bars, hotels, and even the construction deals. Well, until I negotiated that deal with Cartwright and sealed the deal for Dmitri who in turn planned on hiring you guys at Pro-Tech as well as Liberty Construction to do the jobs." She took a breath and continued to explain everything they had been working on, including the last three weeks at Pro-Tech.

"How the hell did you do all of that?" Porter asked.

"How the hell did you know that there are spies in our company?" Winter asked her.

"Well, back to that little visit in Andrei's restaurant in the back room. He told me he had people planted in there ready to sabotage from within, in case he needed to discredit your company. Hence, the one problem you ran into a year ago with the ex-boyfriend hiring your guys to find the girlfriend and kill her. Never mind a few other close calls more recently that I was able to nip in the bud rather quickly. By the way, I'll have a confirmed list to you ASAP when I get access to my laptop upstairs. You can begin firing these assholes pronto. And don't worry, between Dmitri and I we came up with the idea of you hiring more retired military personnel so they can support their families now that they're out of the service."

"Holy fuck. You've been pretending to work for us while pretending to work for Andrei?" York asked, sounding outraged.

She shrugged her shoulders.

"You let that fucker kiss you in his office? He had his hands on you, Aspen?" Zin asked.

"Please calm down. This is going to work out. Dmitri and I have the entire thing figured out. There's just the issue of the Star Haven program Dmitri started and supported. Apparently, Sotoro and a few others like Demyan have been using the program to snag potential employees as well as high-priced hookers. It seems these women have been working in the back rooms of some of Andrei and Demyan's clubs. Clubs that Dmitri is interested in taking over."

"Aspen."

She continued to talk about the list of people she had come up with and about working with Dmitri.

"Aspen."

She looked at Storm since he raised his voice at her.

"All this time, you've been working with Dmitri, uncovering this potential takeover, risking your life in a world that your brother and all of us have been trying to protect you from?" His voice raised on the last word as he stepped toward her. Instinctively she stepped back.

"Let's take this upstairs," Winter said.

"Let's not. I'm seeing fucking red right now, Aspen. Fucking red. Do you have any idea what kind of danger you've placed yourself in by dealing with men like Andrei and Dmitri?" he scolded.

She could tell he was extremely angry and so were the others. They all looked upset with her. "I explained to York and Porter, how I was in a different mind frame until recently." She pulled her bottom lip between her teeth as she shyly looked at her brother then back to Storm, Winter, Zin, York, and Weston.

"I didn't care about living or dying, only seeking revenge. You have no idea what it feels like, what it felt like to know that man was responsible for my abduction, and that he continued to corrupt the innocent of society. I knew exactly what I was getting into. I knew the dangers and I didn't care. All I knew was that I could get Andrei back the best way I knew how to. By hitting him where it hurts. His damn fat wallet. So if you're angry at me, if you think I'm stupid and don't understand exactly why we're here right now, then so be it. My only focus now is saving your company, protecting India and all the men I love, whether you like it or not," she stated firmly as her voice cracked with emotion.

They just stared at her with blank expressions until Storm pointed at her and curled his finger for her to come to him.

Is he serious? Does he actually think I'll walk right into the punishment I'm sure to get for all these crazy stunts I pulled?

"When a made man, a Mafia boss, issues an order to come, you better damn well do it fast," Porter said from behind her.

She glanced up and over her shoulder at her brother. He looked just as firm. Then she noticed he and his team bow their heads toward Storm and then walk from the porch.

Winter cleared his throat and crossed his arms in front of his chest.

Storm raised an eyebrow at her and she found herself walking toward him then stopping a foot or so in front of him.

"Closer," he said firmly.

She swallowed hard and then stood only a few inches in front of him. She bowed her head.

"Look at me," Storm said as the others surrounded her.

She tilted her head up and looked at Storm, then at Winter, then Weston and Zin and finally York.

"You belong to us. You're our woman. As the woman, the wife to made men, there are certain responsibilities, rules that you need to abide by. The most important one is obeying your men's commands so you remain out of danger. I understand your emotions and how you felt. Perhaps if we came forward sooner and expressed our love for you earlier, you wouldn't have been so compelled to risk your neck for revenge against a mob boss."

"She would have been too busy in bed with us to focus on anything else," Zin stated.

"Her actions will not go unpunished." Winter told her as he eyed her body over.

Why she was completely aroused right now she didn't know. But thinking that her brother and his team were only inside the house a short distance away kind of killed her arousal. Well, maybe only a little.

"I accept whatever punishment my men feel is necessary. But just so you know, I would do it again because that's how much I love all of you. We can save your territory. Together."

"We don't care about the territory in Chicago, Aspen. We were willing to give it all up for you and focus our attentions here in Texas, where things are more legit. We had already spoken with Dmitri," Weston told her.

"Dmitri? Why?"

"Dmitri is family. He'll be getting an earful from me soon enough," Storm replied.

"Family? What do you mean?"

"He's my cousin," Storm said.

"So that's why he's been so helpful. He's been keeping an eye on me, too."

Zin pulled her into his arms and held her close, placing his hands over her ass cheeks.

"He'll be reprimanded for that, too. No more private meetings or phone conversations with our wife," Zin told her.

"Wife? What are you talking about?" she asked, feeling excited and hopeful.

"We're getting married. As soon as this is over," Winter said.

"Yeah, we're never going to leave your side, Aspen. Since you're okay with the fact that we have some illegal businesses as well as legal ones, then you won't mind the fact that you need security at all times," Weston told her.

"Since you're so good at ditching the guards we used before, we're going to personally be your bodyguards," York said, and the others smiled.

Winter pulled her into his arms next. "Tonight, after your brother and his team leave, you're going to get your first punishment." He squeezed her ass then gave it a light smack.

"Winter." She gasped and he kissed her deeply.

"Let's get inside and work out some plans. We need to make sure that India is transported to a safe location and not followed," Storm said.

"I'm going to get him back for hurting India," Aspen said aloud, and then Zin stopped her and they all looked at her with firm expressions.

She smiled and hugged Zin's arm as she started walking again. "We're going to get him back for that."

"I think someone is going to have a very sore ass tomorrow," Weston said. They all agreed and chuckled, but Aspen widened her eyes and wondered just how serious the men really were.

* * * *

India could hardly keep her eyes open. Her one eye was so sore. Her lips hurt where she couldn't talk. She felt aches and pains everywhere.

"Come on now, honey. Aspen, Silas, and the guys all want you safe," Dmitri told her as he lifted her up and carried her out of the room. Her eyes ached from the bright lights illuminating the hallway.

"Where am I?" she asked as her eyes adjusted to the light. She inhaled and could smell the antiseptic, and the sanitary, cold aroma of hospital.

"You're in the hospital now but soon you'll be on my private jet and a hell of a lot safer than right here."

"Jet?" she asked and then held on to him as he descended the stairs.

"All clear." She heard another male voice. She sensed Dmitri nodding his head.

He moved faster as a door opened, the metal creaking and then Dmitri cursed.

"Fuck. Take them out. We need a clear escape," he mumbled and then picked up his pace, her bouncing in his arms.

"Hold on, honey." He ran with her. She heard a series of sounds.

Swoosh, swoosh, swoosh.

"Get her inside. We got it covered. Flynn's at the airport waiting," a voice said. It sounded deep, strong, and she blinked her eyes open, but more sounds echoed around them as Dmitri covered her head and tucked her close.

He got her into a truck. Some sort of dark vehicle. The door slammed closed and the sound of tires squealing echoed outside.

"Are you both okay?" another person asked.

"We're good. I can't wait to get these fucking assholes back," Dmitri said in a deep, ominous voice.

"You'll get your chance, Dmitri, and in the interim, we'll do our job. Don't you worry," the other man said.

"Dmitri?" she whispered.

He caressed her hair. "You're going to be safe now, India. Your brother has gotten some of the best men to protect you and keep you safe."

"Protect me?" she asked, feeling herself losing strength to continue speaking.

"Yes, India, you're going somewhere where Andrei and his crew can't hurt you ever again. Now rest. All you need to worry about is getting better."

She held on to him, feeling fearful, shivering in his arms. She hardly even knew Dmitri Sanclare. No one really did. But she knew of him, and she knew how close Aspen was to him. Dmitri said Silas had arranged for her protection. Her brother was in soldier mode. They all probably were. She closed her eyes and prayed that her brother, her best friend, and all the men were safe. Andrei Renoke was a monster, and she hoped that he, Demyan, and especially Iakov got what they deserved.

The only future for the evil mind was death of the most violent kind.

Chapter 7

"Oh please, please, Zin!" Aspen cried out as her pussy wept and her thighs shook. They were all gathered around her on the bed. A bed she was handcuffed to. She was facing forward toward the headboard. Her arms were stretched out in front of her, balancing on her knees and shins, kneeling, her thighs spread wide. She was so overstimulated already and they hadn't even spanked her yet. She stretched her fingers, the soft thick fur protecting her wrists from getting cut or bruised. Never in her wildest dreams had she imagined anything so erotic and wild.

"Oh!" She gasped as Zin tapped his hand against her pussy, lightly arousing her already swollen pussy lips.

The bed dipped again and the feel of thick, hard palms rubbing up her body from ankles to thighs to ass then hips made her shiver with anticipation.

"You've been a very naughty girl, Aspen," Weston whispered into her hair, surprising her as all her attention was on Storm, whose hands made their way around her body, squeezing and spreading her thighs.

"You need to learn discipline, and your place as a wife to made men," Winter told her in her other ear.

"Wife?"

Smack.

"Oh God!" She jerked from the unexpected smack to her ass as well as their continued reference to her as their wife. Her heart pounded. It was filled with emotion, with desire.

Smack.

"Oh!" She moaned again.

"That's right, wife. You're going to be our wife as soon as this shit is over. But right now you concentrate on the feel of our hands on you, possessing you, reminding you that you belong to us, Aspen. You're ours to protect, to love, and we expect respect and submission. Do you submit?" Storm asked her.

She felt the hands on her body everywhere. Fingers grazed her sensitive pussy lips, lips brushed against her lips, and she saw Weston in front of her, naked and stroking his cock. Then York gripped her wrist where the handcuffs met. He locked gazes with her and appeared so dominant and lethal. She shivered and lowered her head but held his gaze. He smirked yet didn't smile. It was in his eyes. He was telling her, they all were, that they owned her, possessed her, protected her, and they were in command.

She felt her pussy clench, and cream dripped down her thighs.

Zin grabbed an ankle on her left side and Winter grabbed an ankle on her right side. She felt their palms stroke up her calves to the backs of her knees. They gripped and parted her thighs wider.

"Oh God, please. Please," she begged. For whatever they were willing to give her. A smack to her ass, a finger to her cunt, she didn't care. She just needed them on her, inside her, making them one.

Storm was right behind her and she felt the palms of his hands caressing her ass. She moaned again.

"You belong to us. Tell us," he ordered in that tone that was all Storm. Her body tightened and she tightened up, too.

Smack, smack, smack.

"I belong to you. To all of you," she blurted out a little too late.

"You don't sound too sure, Aspen," Storm said and then she felt the series of smacks to her ass with caresses of hard, firm palms in between. She wiggled and moaned, receiving spank after spank from his firm hand and then the others spanked her, too.

She felt about ready to lose her mind as tears stung her eyes and a realization hit her so hard she gasped.

"I'm sorry. I love you. I love all of you and I'm yours. Only yours forever!" she screamed, and a thick, blunt finger stroked up her cunt.

"Holy God almighty!" she screamed out and came hard.

A moment later they were all moving. A hand gently gripped her hair and head, causing her to look up and lock gazes with Weston. He nodded his head in approval, making her feel so good inside as he moved the tip of his cock closer to her lips. She wanted him so badly. Wanted to please him, confirm to him, to all of them, that she belonged to them and submitted to them fully. Whatever they told her, asked of her, she would do because she loved them with all her heart.

She opened, accepting the thick, hard muscle and moaning at the first taste of pre-cum on the tip. She twirled around it, but Weston didn't want to hold back, nor did Storm as the cool liquid was pressed to her sensitive anus.

She accepted Weston's cock, relaxing her throat and taking him in. She jerked as Storm nipped her ass cheeks and spread them wide.

"Ours, Aspen. All ours. Every fucking part of you," Storm whispered against her ear then pressed his cock into her ass.

Zin cupped her breasts and tweaked her nipple. York did the same on the other side.

Winter was at the top of the bed to her left next to Weston when she felt his fingers stroke her pussy.

"That's it. Damn, our woman is sopping wet. I need her, too. Fuck, I need her bad," Winter stated.

Storm gripped her hips and pumped into her ass faster.

"Get under there, Winter. She's ours for the taking," Weston told him as he gripped her hair and eased his cock from her mouth.

Winter pulled out his fingers and slid under her as Storm lifted her up by her waist. Weston lifted her handcuffed hands higher and she immediately placed them over Winter's head to rest behind him. Her breasts swayed by his mouth as he adjusted his cock. He licked a nipple and bit gently, tugging on the berry.

A moment later she was impaled on Winter's cock.

"Oh my God. Oh God, I feel so full," she said as she moaned and moved her hips. She began riding him with help from Storm who kept his cock deep in her ass as she adjusted to Winter's invasion.

"There we go. Now that's a fucking sight," Weston said, taking a handful of her hair and drawing her mouth back to his now very hard, thick cock.

"Come on, baby, we're taking you together," Weston said and she felt the need to satisfy them and to submit to their control once again. She opened her mouth and moaned as Winter and Storm began a fast, deep pace into her body, claiming her. She sucked Weston harder and in rhythm to Storm and Winter's thrusts.

"Sweet mother, I can't wait," Zin said, and she felt the slap to her ass on one side and then the slap to her ass from the other side.

Zin and York.

"We'll protect you always. Always, Aspen. We're one now. One," Storm chanted and she felt his cock thicken, her pussy swell, and her own body erupt in an orgasm as they came together. Weston shot his semen down her throat. She swallowed and suckled as her body shook from her own orgasm and from the jerky movements of Storm and Winter as they came inside of her.

Weston pulled from her mouth then kissed her lips and plunged his tongue inside of her mouth.

"I love you, baby. I fucking love you," he said after he released her lips.

She smiled softly. "I love you, too."

Her arms ached and she moaned as Storm pulled from her ass, caressing calves and thighs as he stepped to the side.

He leaned down as she raised up, releasing Winter's cock from her pussy in the motion. He moaned and Storm cupped her cheeks and held her gaze firmly.

"No one will ever have you, touch you, possess you other than the five of us, ever again. You got that?"

He sounded so possessive, demanding, and sexy. She nodded her head, feeling his power and control move over her flesh, making her feel aroused, desired, and special.

He kissed her lips. "I love you, Aspen. Remember that always. No matter where you are or who you're with, know that I love you."

"I love you, too, Storm," she replied.

Winter rolled her to her back and straddled her hips. She could feel his softened cock against her inner thigh as he cupped her face and stared down into her eyes.

"I've never loved a woman before, Aspen. I never knew what love was until you came along. I promise to give you all of me as you've given us all of you. I love you, too," he said.

"I love you right back," she replied, and he winked then kissed her sweetly.

"Well, now it's our turn to love her so move aside, big guy," York said as he and Zin climbed onto the bed. Zin unlocked the handcuffs and then tossed them onto the dresser. He licked across her wrists and kissed her skin but she wasn't tender or sore. She liked the feel of the bindings against her skin from the moment Weston and Winter placed her in them.

Winter chuckled as he moved to the side and off the bed.

She felt York's hand slide up her inner thigh, spreading her wider as he leaned on his side next to her. She turned her head to look at him, absorbed all his muscles, tattoos, and the intense gaze in those gorgeous hazel eyes that mesmerized her so.

"You're so damn special. I don't think you know how special you are, woman. You"—he cupped her pussy, stroking a finger up into her cunt—"complete me." He leaned down and kissed her.

Zin kissed a trail down the skin of her inner arm to her breast, licking the mound and then the nipple. He twirled his tongue around the tiny berry as York thrust two fingers slowly up into her cunt.

"Spread your thighs and offer this body up to us," York said, and she was more than willing to do that. She lifted her pelvis, pushed out her breasts, and widened her thighs as she placed her arms above her head.

Zin chuckled, his warm breath tickling her nipple, making it instantly harden again.

"I think we've got ourselves an obedient lover who loves submitting to her men," Zin said.

"I think she likes being restrained, Zin, and I think I like restraining her," York said as he eased his hand up and locked her wrists together with one strong, muscular hand.

She gasped and felt her pussy leak some more cream.

"Oh yeah, she definitely likes being restrained," Winter chimed in then pulled a seat closer to the bed.

She looked downward, chin to chest, and saw that Weston, Winter and Storm now watched to see what Zin and York would do to her.

It aroused her so much that she came, shaking and moaning.

"Hot damn, she likes an audience, too," Weston added, and the three of them chuckled. But Zin and York looked intensely serious.

"Zin, grab the blindfold," York said.

The men made comments. "Oh yeah, here we go," Weston stated aloud and clapped his hands before rubbing them together and sitting forward in the chair.

She felt her nipples tighten and her core ache with desire. She was just as turned on as they were.

Zin got up and returned quickly with a long black piece of silk. He placed it over her eyes and tied it behind her head.

"Listen to the sound of our voices, and the feel of our hands touching you. Don't move or make a sound," York told her.

It was wild, but the moment the blindfold was placed over her eyes, she felt so helpless, yet she sought out Zin and York for support and guidance.

"We're right here, baby. Right here. All of us," Zin said as they moved her to the edge of the bed and helped her to stand.

"Spread your thighs. Widen that stance," Storm commanded. She gulped and did just that. Her belly tightened and she wrapped an arm around her waist.

"No. Place your arms and hands up behind your head like you're under arrest," Zin said and she slowly moved her arms above her head and behind.

There was complete silence—no sound, no movement, nothing—and it made her body hum with something she didn't recognize. It wasn't fear or insecurity but an inner arousal at knowing her men all watched her standing there blindfolded, naked, and submissive to all of them. It turned her on and made her feel desperate. Yes, desperate for their touch, their voices, anything for them.

She squirmed when she felt the warm breath collide against her pussy. Instinctively she looked down, beginning to close her legs when she felt the light slap to her pussy.

"Stay open," York said, and she gulped.

Fingers collided against her inner groin on both sides, but she could tell they weren't fingers from the same person. The idea of two of them touching her together brought on a surge of arousal again.

"Fuck, you're so wet, baby," Zin said.

She felt one finger press up into her cunt and then come out. Before she could protest, another finger pressed up into her cunt then came out. They continued to torment her, one stroke after the next until she felt the lick to her nipple on one side then the tug of her nipple on the other side. She moaned aloud.

"Oh God, that feels so good. My legs are shaking," she admitted.

Hands glided up and down her thighs to her ass. She was surrounded by muscles, power, and manliness. She couldn't focus on one sensation as her mind and her body reacted to every touch. The nip to her ass, the slap to her pussy, the thrust of fingers, then the feel of his mouth over her nipples.

She began to rock and thrust her hips. She could feel herself begin to lose control, as the orgasm was only a tiny bit away.

"Oh God, please, please don't stop."

All touching ceased She was pulled backward and felt like she would fall into oblivion, which seemed to heighten her arousal more as her back hit the mattress. Her thighs were parted and a cock slapped against her needy cunt.

"Oh." She reached out and hands gripped her wrists.

"Keep them up there, baby. Tell me how badly you want a cock in you."

"Badly. Badly." She moaned.

York tapped his thick, hard cock against her wet, swollen pussy lips and she wiggled and swayed.

"Please, York, please take me. Fuck me, damn it!" she yelled, and chuckles spread through the room. She felt a bit embarrassed but instantly that emotion changed to pleasurable shock as York spread her thighs and sunk his cock into her to the hilt.

He moaned and she screamed out. "Holy God, you feel so big. Oh God, York, I can't take it."

He pounded into her, holding her by her arms and rocking his hips into her pussy.

"You're perfect, Aspen. So beautiful and so fucking perfect." He kissed her mouth and then ran his hands up and down her arms as he stroked his cock in and out of her. She felt the heaviness of his masculine body collide against hers as her legs hung over the edge of the bed. She was chanting for him to continue when he paused, rolled to the side, and she nearly fell off-balance as she landed on top of him.

Hands gripped her hips and cool liquid spread over her anus then up into her ass. "Fuck, you drive me crazy, baby. I'm going to fuck this ass so good and hard. Do you want that? Do you want my hard cock fucking your ass?" Zin asked her.

"Yes. Yes do it now. Do it, Zin, now." She sounded so wild and carnal and something came over her as she increased her thrusts over

York. Her breasts bounced, her groin grinded against his cock, and she could feel York's balls under her ass.

Zin spread her wider, stroking his fingers in and out of her ass, then pulled out. She wanted to scream for him to get back in there when she felt the top of his thick cock against the tight puckered hole and then him shove into her deeply.

She screamed out and York moaned then cupped her breasts, pulled on the nipples, and then pulled her closer to him. "You feel so fucking good."

She tore the blindfold from her eyes and grabbed onto his shoulders and joined them rocking and thrusting.

They moaned and chanted. She felt her body tighten and she convulsed between them, screaming out until her voice was hoarse. Zin and York continued to stroke into her ass and pussy, relentlessly trying to find their release. The bed rocked and the room spun as they came hard and fast, holding their cocks deep within her as they shook.

"I love you so fucking much, baby. Damn, that was fucking incredible," York said, cupping her cheeks and kissing her deeply.

"I love you, too." She panted once he released her.

Behind her, Zin caressed her ass cheeks and gave them two slaps.

"I love fucking this ass, and I love you, baby. You're a pleasant surprise." He pulled out of her then knelt on the bed, took her face between his hands, and kissed her deeply.

Once he released her, she smiled. "I love you, too, but I think I'm going to pass out."

York chuckled as he pulled out and rolled her to her back.

She closed her eyes, feeling the warm washcloth and the gentle kisses to her skin as she lay there spent and helpless. But she didn't have a care in the world or a worry. Her five men were there, her American soldiers, her made men who loved her and would protect her forever.

* * * *

The next few days were hard on all of them. As the men began to clean house at Pro-Tech Industries, Aspen worked on securing and organizing the job with Cartwright. Her men forbid her to have any more involvement in taking down Andrei. They explained that it was part of their illegal business side and they didn't want her connected legally if anything went wrong. They had taken the time to explain to her about their connections to the Russian Mafia, as well as other organized crime syndicates. She was shocked to learn that it was Storm who was related to Dmitri and it wasn't difficult to figure out that his family name was quite important. He'd continued to go by his mother's maiden last name to hide his identity when he went into the military. That had been his calling in life.

But Winter explained that they all came from troubled pasts and the military was their way of surviving, getting three square meals a day, and belonging to a family that wouldn't disappoint them and always had their backs. Zin expressed the love he had for the men he considered his brothers. York told her about how life had been when they retired from the military and how difficult of a time they all had adapting to civilian life, finding work they liked and that paid well, and how they almost gave up. Weston explained about the jobs they took at first and then the ones as the muscle for loan sharks that were connected to Storm's family businesses. She felt badly for them as they referred to themselves as orphans who'd found one another and formed a family, a bond that could never be broken.

She was impressed and touched by the deep connection. She also felt a bit jealous of that. She'd never had a mother because she died when Aspen was just an infant. Her father, what she remembered of him, was always angry, always combative, and then he got sick and was even more miserable. If not for Porter, Aspen may not have learned to survive on her own and be so independent. But she had no choice. In the city it was do or die. Fight for a better life, for better things or succumb to the easy way out.

She'd always had this inner strength, this fight in her, and she often wondered if it came from her mother. From what she remembered about her father and what Porter told her about him, it didn't seem to come from him. Fighting for survival and a better life wasn't the same as fighting to hurt someone and keep them at bay.

She heard the knock at her door and was surprised to see Pamela there. The woman, despite Aspen's concern that she was working for Andrei, had come up clean. There was no real evidence indicating Pamela was on the take.

"Hi, Pamela, what's going on?"

"I was just wondering if you wanted to do lunch."

"Oh, I'm not sure. I think York was coming down to go with me."

"I don't think so. Alex from security just said that York and the guys were meeting someone from Sparks Industries upstairs in the boardroom."

"Oh, they must have secured the meeting after all. Great. Then I guess I am free, but we have to have it downstairs in the café. Is that okay?"

"Great for me. I have been dying to try that pumpkin spice latte. I heard it is so good. I might even get it with cream instead of skim milk," Pamela said, rubbing her hands together.

Aspen chuckled. "Sounds delicious. I think I'll join you. Let me just grab my bag and text the guys."

She reached for her phone and texted Weston. He was supposed to be working in his office on data sheets and numbers for the materials needed on the Cartwright job.

She turned off her desk light and headed out of the room, closing her office door behind her. Pamela pressed the button on the elevator. They waited patiently as they chatted about the new boutique opening in town and the art gallery showing new work. Aspen explained about knowing Gia and her friend Mariana and how they were in charge of the art and owned the gallery.

"I don't think this damn elevator is working. Let's take the stairs. Then I can definitely have the cream in that latte. This will count as a workout," Pamela said as they entered the stairwell.

They were laughing, talking about exercising and the demands on women to look good in certain outfits as they came to the lobby floor entrance.

Aspen went to open the door when she felt a prick to her neck.

She gasped and turned around to see Pamela with the needle in her hand. "Pamela, why?" she asked as she fell against the metal door but didn't fall to the floor. Aspen held on to the door, searching for the handle as the sound of footsteps thumped from the stairwell below.

Pamela gave her the once-over. "They were mine and you came here and took them. Now I'll comfort them when they find your body and know you're dead. They'll be all mine."

The anger filled Aspen's belly and then the shock as she saw the two men appear behind Pamela. Aspen was enraged as she swung her fist into Pamela's face, breaking her nose.

Pamela screamed out as the two men grabbed Aspen and yanked her down the stairs. She was losing her ability to stand and stay conscious. What had Pamela stuck her with?

She tried fighting off the men but couldn't. She was getting so weak, her legs gave out and then the one guy lifted her up over his shoulder. They pushed open the back door and hurried down the metal stairs to an awaiting van. They tossed her inside, and then they jumped into the front and sped off. She banged on the door and tried to pull it open but it wouldn't budge.

She was losing focus more and more, but fighting it and trying to think. She grabbed onto her purse that she had over her shoulder. Her cell phone.

The van sped ahead and the men only looked over their shoulder at her a few times through the divider window.

She opened the phone as she fell on her side, her eyes blurry, tears streaming down her cheeks. She could hardly press the buttons.

"Hello? Aspen?"

She heard Storm's voice.

"Help me," she said as the van swerved to the left, causing her to slide to the right and release the phone before darkness overtook her.

* * * *

"Aspen! Aspen!" Storm yelled out in the boardroom. They were all there, including the man who owned Sparks Industries now, on the speakerphone. The one remaining anonymous to everyone but Storm.

He looked at his team and the others. He hit speaker so they could hear.

The sound of Russian voices filtered through the phone.

"Who the fuck is that? They have Aspen?" Winter asked.

Storm covered his mouth with his fingers, indicating for Winter and the others to remain quiet.

"That's Romanian and Russian mixed. That has to be Andrei's guys," Zin said.

He heard the man's voice on the other end of the speaker ask what was going on.

"Someone took her. They have Aspen," Storm stated.

The speakerphone clicked off and Storm started giving orders as he held the phone out so his team and the others in the room could still listen.

He handed the phone to Weston.

"You listen carefully to this. See if they give any indication as to where they took Aspen." Weston nodded as he took the phone and walked to the other room where it was quiet.

"What are we going to do?" York asked.

"That fucking bastard is not going to take our woman from us. He'll die before he even gets the chance."

Winter's phone rang and he answered it.

He looked at Storm.

"It's Andrei." He placed it on speaker.

"Give up your territory, Sparks Industries, and Pro-Tech, or your sweet Aspen will succumb to her fate after all."

"You let her go now, Andrei. You fucking let her go!" York yelled out.

"What the fuck do you mean succumb to her fate?" Storm asked.

"She's a very beautiful woman. Has a body men would pay a very high price for," Andrei told them.

"You motherfucker. I'm going to kill you, Andrei. When I get my hands on you, it will bring me great pleasure to squeeze the life from you and watch you die."

"*Poshel na khuy!*"

"No, fuck you. You want a blood war? You've got yourself a fucking blood war." Storm disconnected the call. "I want everyone we've got. Get on the phone with Dmitri, Zin."

"I'm on it," Zin replied.

"We're doing this? You know what it will mean? No more focusing on going completely legit?" York asked.

"We have no choice. Aspen means more than anything else, but the only way to save her is to take on Andrei and win."

Weston ran into the room. "They're taking her on a plane. They're going to Mexico."

"Motherfuckers! They're bringing her back to where she was ten years ago. That sick fuck knows what this will do to Aspen. He knows she won't be able to handle this a second time!" Zin yelled.

"He said she would succumb to her fate. We don't have time for anything else but to get to Aspen. This time she'll be sold as a sex slave. He plans on succeeding," Storm replied.

"Fuck!" York yelled out.

"Storm, security found Pamela in the stairwell. Her nose is broken and she's all messed up. She said there were two men waiting in the lower stairwell, and she tried to fight them with Aspen, but she couldn't."

"Get her an ambulance," Zin said.

As Winter headed out of the room with his phone to his ear, Storm called out.

"Wait. Why the hell didn't they take the elevator? Where would Aspen be going with Pamela?" he asked.

"She came up clean remember? Do you really think Pamela was involved?" Winter asked. Storm raised one eyebrow up.

"Aspen felt so. Even after the reports came back. Get some video. Check with them while York calls the airport and gets the plane ready."

Winter saluted and left the room. York pulled out his phone and called the private airport to get the jet ready.

Zin Looked at Storm. "We let our guard down. They took her right out from under our noses. Right here at the company."

"We'll get her back. She's smart, she's stronger than before, and she had the know-how to make the phone call. As long as we keep that signal and can verify her location, we'll get to her in time. It's time to use all our resources, Zin. We may be made men, but we'll always be American soldiers. Let's do what we do best. Hunt down the enemy and take them out. This time, once and for all."

Chapter 8

Aspen awoke in time to be dropped on the concrete floor. She reacted on instincts and swung her fist at the man who dropped her, but her arm came right back at her. She was chained to some post like a dog.

"Let me go. You'll never get away with this!" she screamed at them.

The blow to her side by a boot shocked her. She cried out and rolled to the left but the chains brought her back over.

"She's a wild one. I think she needs to be broken in before the sale," the one man said in his thick Russian accent. He had a beard, a big belly, and was filled with muscles.

"Leave the breaking in for me. Leave us be. The boat is fueling up. We leave in fifteen minutes."

She turned toward that voice and knew who it was immediately. Iakov that Russian piece of crap. He was the one who tried to sell her when she was seventeen. Dread filled her belly and made her feel sick. She wasn't going to make it out alive this time. Storm, Winter, Zin, York, and Weston were not going to be able to rescue her. Andrei and Iakov were different. They were smarter now and knew what to do to succeed in destroying Storm. They would gain his territory. They would use her to make him hand it all over as they threatened to kill her. But once it was done they would say she was long gone. Sold to some sick fuck with deep pockets who had to buy women held hostage by men like Iakov and Andrei. They deserved to die a sick death. If she had a chance, she would take it and kill them herself. Even if it cost her own life.

Iakov took a deep breath and released it as he squatted down next to her thighs.

He reached over and she jerked her leg free. He widened his eyes at her. "It would serve you better to be obedient. Perhaps there would be room to negotiate who will buy you."

What was he saying? That he would buy her? That she would be his sex slave? She would rather die a thousand deaths than succumb to his touch, his possession.

"You need to cooperate, Aspen. If we have to mess up this pretty face and this sexy body, some shady characters will be the only ones interested in purchasing you."

"You're sick!" she yelled at him and tried pulling away only to lose her balance from the chains binding her to the concrete as she fell to her side. In a flash he gripped her hips and straddled her.

She felt the pain on her back as it scraped against the concrete. He gripped her throat, her arms reaching out to stop him but then came right back to the concrete because of the short chains she was attached to. Pain radiated through her arms and her shoulders.

Iakov smirked. He trailed a finger over her lips as he maintained his hold on her neck with his other hand.

"You will go for a very high price, Aspen. You know why?" he asked her.

She felt the tears sting her eyes. Iakov was a monster. He was enjoying this.

"Because you like to get fucked in every hole. There's no need to ease you into it. The man or men who get to have you will probably tie you to a bed, or maybe just to a pole, and have their way with you whenever the urge is there."

He cupped her breast and squeezed it.

"No! No, you can't do this. Stop. Stop it please!" she cried out.

"There are three men right now in the running to make you theirs." He continued to play with her body and do what he wanted. She cried and felt like vomiting.

"One wants you for himself. He likes to use whips and chains to ensure his slaves are obedient. They don't last long though. A week tops, before they die from his actions."

She whimpered as he pinched and pulled on her breast.

"The other likes to share, too. Something you've grown accustomed to over the last several weeks, from what my sources say."

She didn't want to hear any more. She couldn't take it as tears streamed down her cheeks.

She needed to change the subject, and get him to stop torturing her body.

"What sources?" she asked, voice quivering.

"Ahh…just a few individuals working at your lovers' company." He lifted up so he could push his hand under her dress and up her thigh. She tried wiggling away, and he thrust downward on her, making her hip and back ache from the heavy weight of his body. He squeezed her throat tighter and she couldn't fend him off, being restrained like this. Her wrists burned as the skin broke and she began to bleed.

She felt his hand move up her thigh to her mound.

"You know Pamela," he told her. That woman was a conniving liar. She hoped that her men saw through her lies and knew that Pamela aided in her abduction. They would look at the surveillance tapes. They would see the truth right there. But if Pamela blocked those cameras somehow, the men wouldn't know the truth. She worried that they might believe her and fall victim to Pamela's lies. If Aspen died, would Pamela get her claws into the five men Aspen loved with all her heart?

"Oh I know her. I broke her fucking nose, the weak bitch." Aspen spat at him, and Iakov rose up and slapped her face. Blood dripped from her cracked lip and she cried in pain.

"Iakov, the boat is ready!" one of his men yelled to him from the doorway.

He stood up then reached in his pocket to grab a key.

"You're not so tough now are you?" he asked, and when he bent down to place the key in the lock by her head, she head-butted him. Blood splattered everywhere, even on her face. He grabbed his nose and yelled in anger before he retaliated.

He unlocked the lock, lifted her up, and shoved her forward. She fell to her knees, scraping them as he kicked her and yelled at her to move faster.

She gasped for air from the strikes to her ribs but knew she needed to make a move before they got her to the dock.

She saw the piece of metal bar and grabbed for it.

He pulled a gun and she swung with all her might.

The gun fired, missing her, but she didn't miss him. He fell over and she ran, picking up the gun but then dropping it because of the bindings on her wrists. She needed that gun, and she struggled to pick it up best she could with the bindings still in place. She looked around quickly then ran the other way away from the dock and boats.

She didn't know where to go when she heard yelling in Russian, then some sort of commotion outside and behind her. She was out of breath, unable to get enough oxygen into her lungs because of the pain in her ribs. She knew they must be broken.

She dodged between large wooden crates and ducked down catching her breath.

She checked the gun. It was fully loaded minus the one shot Iakov had taken at her. But there weren't enough to take out all the guards around the place. She needed to get out of here quickly.

Aspen slowly backstepped farther and farther from the entrance to the boat dock.

"Where do you think you're going, sweetheart?" The huge Russian with the muscles and beard grabbed her by the shoulders. He turned her around, and she went to point the gun when he slugged her in the belly. She fell to the ground, holding the gun as he yelled out that he found her. She couldn't let Iakov get to her. She couldn't let him take her on that ship.

She gripped the gun and trigger, and he turned her over and she shot him.

He gasped and grabbed his stomach as she scooted backward, back onto her feet, experiencing even more difficulty breathing. She knocked over some boxes as she struggled to move straight and not off-balance.

Someone gripped her hair and pulled her back.

"No!" she screamed out as Iakov dragged her across the concrete and in between boxes, kicking and screaming.

He got her close to the dock where the large boat was when he let go of her hair.

She turned, rolled, and tried scrambling away when she felt the strike to her back. He pulled her up and she knew this was it. She needed to fight him off or die here. She wasn't going on that ship.

He struck her again and she continued fighting him until she no longer had the strength. He dragged her onto the wooden dock, her legs scraping, filling with splinters of old wood sticking out of the dock. She didn't want to be sold. She didn't want to go on the boat and never see her men again. But no one was coming. Andrei and Iakov had succeeded.

He pulled her up toward the ramp, dragging her kicking and screaming when she heard the commotion.

She recognized the sounds immediately and held on to the metal bar of the ramp.

Swoosh, swoosh, swoosh.

Around her bullets hit the guards, the metal bar where she was, and right next to Iakov. He pulled his gun from his waist and knocked her in the head with it.

He then fired back. She was losing focus. The blow was too much as blood dripped from her temple.

More men went down.

Iakov's body jerked as bullet after bullet hit him and he grabbed her throat and fell over the edge of the boat ram, taking her with him.

* * * *

Nicolai Merkovicz had come through. Someway, somehow, he alerted Storm and his men to Aspen's location and got them there pronto. Storm didn't know if the head of the Russian mob just cared about Storm and the team so much that he wanted to help, or if there was something in it for him. Storm really didn't care. He owed the man his life anyway, and now he would owe him Aspen's if they got her out of there in time. If it weren't for Nicolai, Storm would have gotten killed years ago before he entered the military. With Storm's family connections, he was up for a high position in the Russian Mafia based on his father's name. But Storm wanted nothing to do with that life and instead joined the military to escape it all. Word got out and one of their family's enemies decided to ensure Storm never changed his mind about his position and went to kill him. Storm would never forget that night. He was as good as dead. The gun to his head, the man, Senok Slovonich, had nothing but hatred in his eyes.

The almost silent shots hissed through the air, taking Senok out and saving Storm's life.

Storm had looked up in the direction the bullets came from and saw Nicolai Merkovicz putting away his gun. He was walking away as if he was out for a stroll and hadn't just blown a man's head to pieces. Strom knew that he would never be severed from his ties with the Mafia, but he had a calling. He wanted to serve his country, and being a soldier became his life.

They heard her screams, could see her being dragged across the wooden boardwalk all battered and bruised, her clothing ripped and torn. She had put up a hell of a fight, and still now, appearing seriously injured, she continued to fight.

He gave the hand signal from the water below. They had swum up, using their abilities as Navy SEALs to infiltrate the vicinity along with the rest of the team and their friends they'd called in for backup. Porter had his team infiltrate from land.

As they shot their silencers, being sure not to alert any authorities to their presence, they began to take out each guard one by one.

Storm and his team had perfect aim on Iakov, and as he struck Aspen with the butt of the gun, they took their shot.

He grabbed onto Aspen, her head bleeding from the blow, and fell overboard.

He didn't even have to issue the order as they went underwater, swimming to her as fast as possible. It was pitch black in the water as night overtook the harbor near Brownsville, Texas. The boat was heading toward Mexico and a final destination of Monterrey.

Storm used his special underwater night-vision goggles to locate her as did his team. Zin got to her first and brought her up to the surface.

"She's not breathing!" he yelled out. "Bring her here. Lift her up."

Winter called out as he and York swam quickly to the dock and used their height and muscles to reach up to the high post and pull them up. Then they made a body ramp to lift Aspen up so they could provide first aid to her on the dock.

The others climbed up, including Storm, with a helping hand from Weston.

Winter began chest compressions. Weston cleared her passageway and began mouth-to-mouth resuscitation.

York, Zin, and Storm kept their guns drawn as they made sure no bad guys were coming. Storm communicated with Porter and his team as they headed toward them.

"Come on, baby, breathe damn you. Breathe," Winter cursed at her.

"Come on, sis. Come on now," Porter stated firmly as he fell to his knees and watched.

The sound of her coughing then choking up water as Winter and Weston rolled her to her side was the most amazing sound.

"Fuck yeah, she's tough as nails," Zin stated, sounding proud.

She moaned and held her head.

"Easy, baby. We've got you. But we need to haul ass before the law shows up."

"Winter?" she whispered.

"Yup. Weston has you. We're all here," he said as Weston lifted her up into his arms.

"Let's move now," York said from down in the water. They eased her down and all surrounded her.

"You need to hold on to Weston's neck. I'll be right behind you. Then we'll get to the boat," York told her.

"I don't know if I can. I think I'm going to pass out or puke," she said.

Storm swam up behind her. They were already moving.

"Don't you dare pass out, soldier. That's a direct order. Suck it up and move damn it," Storm ordered. She closed her mouth and held on.

They all swam out of there and to the awaiting motorized blow-up boats they had waiting in the distance.

They climbed in and pulled Aspen up and onto the boat.

"Now you can pass out," Storm told her. She closed her eyes and he could see the bruising, the blood oozing from her head.

"We're going to need an ambulance," Weston said as he held Aspen between his legs.

"No need. There'll be help waiting for us as soon as we get to the location again," Storm told them.

"Who the hell have you been communicating with? Dmitri?" Zin asked.

"Nicolai," Storm said and everyone became silent.

It was York who whistled. "Holy fuck, you do have friends in low places and high ones."

After that no one said a word. Storm hoped Aspen would be okay now as they prepared for the next steps of taking over Andrei Renoke's territory, too.

Chapter 9

Storm stood outside of the room where Aspen was being treated. It wasn't a medical facility. More like an abandoned building with secret rooms set up for emergency medical situations needed by the Russian mob boss Nicolai.

He ran his hands over his face, feeling the stubble and the need for a shower and shave.

"This place is something else," York said.

"Yeah, we could have used this type of place in the service when on a mission. Maybe you wouldn't have gotten that damn infection, Zin, that nearly fucking killed ya," Weston added, and they all mumbled about that.

Storm chuckled. "We've been through a lot together."

"We sure have. And we always come through in one piece," Winter added.

"But the question is, what will you do now that you have this woman to protect?"

They turned to see Nicolai Merkovicz and his guard, Karlicov Lenvick, heading toward them.

They all stood straighter and bowed their heads toward the head of the Russian Mafia family. Storm's team knew that his own family was connected to the Merkovicz family.

Nicolai smiled as he placed his hand on Storm's shoulder. "Your woman is good? She's tough, handled herself well as she bought you time to save her."

Storm nodded his head. He knew that the Russian had knowledge of the answers already. They didn't even have to explain what happened.

"I owe you so much, Nicolai."

He nodded his head and pulled his hand away from Storm's shoulder.

"You have great decision to make, Storm, for your team and your woman. Dmitri has some ideas. Things may be able to be worked out differently."

"Differently?" Storm asked him.

"For family," he said and began to walk toward the room where Aspen was.

"Family, Nicolai? What do you mean? My team and I don't have a choice. Andrei took off. He gave up possession of his territory and the members of the family have already denounced him and placed my name as the new owner."

"It is not final yet, Storm. There is more at stake here. More decisions to make. Come, I want to see for myself that Aspen is okay."

They all followed Nicolai into the room. The moment he entered, the medical staff bowed their heads and the doctor winked and nodded at Nicolai.

They exited the room, leaving Storm, Winter, Zin, York, Weston, and Nicolai gathered around Aspen.

Karlikov stood by the doorway, on guard even here.

Nicolai walked closer. He cursed under his breath and then moved closer and caressed her hair.

Storm's gut tightened and one look at the others and he felt their concern, too.

"Nicolai?"

"She is very beautiful. The bruises will heal," he whispered and then lifted his hand to his lips, kissed them, and then placed his hand to Aspen's forehead.

He turned to look at all of them. "I will give you time to discuss your options with Aspen. You're a team, a family, and I know that you will do what's best for her. But don't be surprised if she doesn't want you to give it all up for her. It may just be in her blood to be the wife of made men. Oh, and marry her as quickly as possible. That will keep enemies at bay. There will be a lot of conflict still. People who worked for Andrei and Iakov who want to remain in their positions and power. But again, you take the time to decide what is right for you."

"Nicolai, what do you mean by saying it's in her blood?"

He looked at each of them and then at Karlikov and back to Aspen.

He touched her hand and squeezed it.

"She has my blood running through her veins. She will make an exceptional wife."

* * * *

"What?" Winter asked, shocked by what Nicolai was saying. He knew that Aspen's mother died when she was an infant, but the woman was married to Porter's father.

"Her mother and I knew one another very well. Our families were of different social classes, but we were in love. I was forced into the life I still lead now and one that Nala's parents didn't want her to be part of. She married Porter's father. They had Porter, but things between them changed. She was going to divorce him. Porter's father suspected that I was seeing Nala and wanted her. He threatened Nala and she denied our involvement together. Nala and I saw one another. She got pregnant with Aspen and was going to leave her husband when someone threatened her, Porter, and the unborn child.

"She gave birth to Aspen, and I had planned to take Aspen, Nala, and Porter in and care for them. Their father found out, and Nala and the baby were used against me in a decision I had to make for the family. But before I could even make the choice, Nala tried to lure the men away from her home so that Aspen and Porter would be safe, when she was killed.

"Her husband never knew that Aspen was mine, but probably figured it out as soon as she grew older. There's no resemblance to him whatsoever. She's mine. I kept her and Porter safe over those years and had my own family watching over her and Porter and keeping eyes on Porter's father. But he was a cruel evil man who died knowing that he had caused his wife's death."

"My God. Porter and Aspen don't know any of this?" Winter asked him.

Nicolai shook his head. "I suppose one day we will need to tell them. But for now I leave Aspen in your hands. Do not fail her ever. Let me know your decision."

Nicolai and Karlicov left the room, and Winter looked at the others.

"What are we going to do?" Winter asked.

"What's best for Aspen. Just like always," Zin stated.

"It's a lot to decide on," Weston said.

"We do like Nicolai asked and we discuss it with Aspen," York added.

"We may have no choice in the matter. Andrei isn't dead. He just disappeared. We'll always worry that he will seek revenge and come after Aspen again. Protecting her and maintaining control and power may be our only option," Storm told them, and they nodded their heads and looked at Aspen.

York covered her hand and smiled. "Are you going to tell her about Nicolai?" York asked Storm.

"She deserves to know. Besides, if she accepts our hands in marriage, then the bloodlines cross and we'd automatically marry into the largest, strongest leader of the Russian mob."

"Holy fuck. Then the decision is made," Zin added.

"Unless Aspen doesn't want that life. We give it all up for her. For love," Storm said.

"All I care about is loving Aspen and keeping her safe and all ours to enjoy and cherish," Winter said.

"Agreed," Zin stated.

"Agreed," they all said as they watched over her.

* * * *

Aspen stared at her five loving men as they gathered in their bedroom at home in Salvation. They had explained so much to her that her head was spinning. She had a million questions, but the two on top of her mind were about her father and about their decision to continue their lives both legit and not so legit.

"Will he ever want to see me and acknowledge that I'm truly his daughter?" she asked them.

Weston caressed her cheek and swallowed hard. "It all depends on the decision we make. If we all agree to continue this life half legit, half not, and take our rightful places in the family, then all will know that you are the daughter of Nicolai Merkovicz," Winter said.

"If we decline it all and give it up to Dmitri, and just focus on our businesses that are legit, then there's hope that we could live a normal life. However, there will always be that threat of Andrei returning to seek his revenge. Even now, we can't exactly stop the connections as we're trying to clean house of Andrei's messes," York added.

"I don't see why you all need to stop doing what has been your lives for many years. It took a lot of hard work to get where you are today. This is your family's reputation, too, Storm. I don't have a problem being under your protection and under guard if you all decide to expand your territory. I just hope that you won't engage in some of the things Andrei did for money. I'm not naive. I get what goes on and that this is a dangerous life. That you all could wind up behind bars or dead. But I also know we make a great team. I don't want to worry about Andrei returning and gaining power. Maybe my father is right. Maybe it's in my blood. I love each of you so much," Aspen told them.

"We love you, too. But I was thinking that maybe we can still go more legit than not. The territory is huge. Dmitri, being my cousin and all, can handle a lot of it on his own. Things like this have been done for generations. I think letting other family members hold on to the control on the front would work perfectly, while we remain in the background, but have the final say," Storm said.

"It's the best of both worlds, and we still get to make sure things are done right, and that no one can infiltrate our empire," Weston added.

"I'm in," Zin said.

"Me, too," York added and they all agreed that they would handle it this way.

Storm leaned closer to Aspen and kissed her shoulder. "So, how does it feel to be a Mafia princess?" he teased.

She lowered down onto the bed, taking Storm with her. "I bet not as great as it will feel being a Mafia queen," she teased and they chuckled.

"There are some tests you have to pass in order to claim such a position," Winter told her then pulled off his shirt.

"Tests?" she asked.

"Oh yeah. Starting with obedience and submission," Weston added then pulled her arms up above her head and held them there. He kissed her wrists where the bandages lay as she lifted her rear, letting Zin pull off her shorts.

"Let's see how obedient our Russian princess can be," York teased.

"Aspen, spread your thighs and show me you're ready for cock," Storm told her.

She slowly spread her thighs and then thrust her pelvis upward.

"Oh yeah, I think she's ready," Winter stated.

Weston kissed her on the mouth as Storm and Winter undressed. Storm lowered to his belly between her legs.

"Get ready, woman, this testing is going to take all fucking night."

Aspen moaned the moment Storm's mouth locked onto her cunt. She thrust and wiggled as they all prepared her body for their cocks.

When he pulled back, she moaned and protested.

Weston released her hands as Winter rolled to his back. Storm placed her on top of Winter, and she immediately sank onto his cock. She gripped his shoulders and rocked her hips.

"How's this?" she asked him as she lowered to his mouth, kissed Winter, then thrust her ass back against Storm's fingers.

"Fucking perfect," Winter said.

"Almost perfect," Weston added as he knelt closer, pulling Aspen toward his cock for her to suck. Aspen pulled it into her mouth as she felt Storm press lube to her ass.

She moaned and Weston grabbed her hair and head before he began a series of slow thrusts into her mouth.

"Oh God, baby, slow down or I'll come before Storm fills your ass," Weston complained, but Aspen kept moaning and sucking.

Smack, smack, smack.

"Oh." She moaned, releasing Weston's cock.

"Submission and obedience," Storm reminded her as Weston aligned his cock with her mouth and she opened just as Storm pressed his cock into her ass.

She was on fire. Could feel her body tighten immediately. She loved them so much she didn't think she could ever live without them in her life.

They moved in sync, thrusting, rocking, filling her up, and claiming her as theirs for eternity.

She counterthrust then hummed and suckled Weston's dick harder. Weston grabbed her hair and thrust deeper, coming inside her mouth. She swallowed and suckled until he cursed and fell backward to the bed.

Storm stroked deeper, faster as the bed dipped and Zin was there holding his cock in his hand. Aspen moved toward it and licked the tip then his balls as Winter watched.

"That is one sexy tongue you got, woman. Suck him good. Don't stop," Winter cheered her on.

She pulled Zin's cock between her lips and sucked him deep as Winter and Storm continued to make love to her.

Then Winter thrust faster, somehow rocking his hips, using his sexy thigh muscles to shove upward. Behind her Storm grew thicker and she felt herself begin to tighten. Storm gripped her hips and came hard, holding himself deep within her. Aspen followed but Zin held her with his cock in her mouth as she came and rocked her hips.

Behind her Storm pulled out and York took his place. He shoved into her ass in one smooth stroke just as Zin exploded into her mouth. It was wild and she didn't know what to focus on as she let her body go and just give in to their demands and their cocks.

She screamed another release as Winter and York fucked her together at record speed. The bed rocked and creaked, her breasts swaying and bouncing, as she cried out in ecstasy just as Winter and York came at the same time.

They began kissing her and caressing her, and after the men pulled from her body, Storm and Zin returned with Weston and cleaned her up then tucked her into bed.

She rolled to her side and took Weston's hand into her own and hugged it to her chest.

"Did I pass?" she whispered. They chuckled.

"The testing phase could take quite some time, Aspen. I think a few tests a day for the next several weeks would be a good indicator," Zin told her. She gasped then threw the pillow at him.

"I think that sounds like a great idea. I could definitely do this multiple times a day for the rest of my life," Weston added.

"I'm in," Winter said from behind her on the bed.

"You don't have to twist my arm," Storm told her.

She looked at York.

He placed his hands on his cock which was already hard again and gave her a sideways expression. "Are you kidding me? Do you really need to ask?"

They all laughed and Aspen shook her head. "You do know that the testing goes both ways?"

"What?" Zin asked her.

"Oh yeah, I have to be sure that the five of you have what it takes to satisfy me every day, multiple times, for the rest of our lives."

"A piece of cake," Weston said.

"Baby, it will be our pleasure to prove that to you, but I think you may have forgotten who we are," York told her.

She eyed them over and licked her lips. "I know who you are. You're made men, you're Navy SEALs, the loves of my life, and my very own little army of American soldiers. But, it's going to take some serious battleground testing to make sure you're more than capable of maintaining this here territory."

Hunger filled their eyes and the sheet was torn from her body, making her gasp.

"Game on, baby. You're about to get real wet, Navy SEAL style." Aspen moaned as excitement and arousal filled her body and happiness overtook her heart.

Life was filled with risks and life-or-death situations. But no matter what their future brought them, they would never regret choosing true love. That was one thing so powerful it wasn't worth compromising at all.

THE END

WWW.DIXIELYNNDWYER.COM

ABOUT THE AUTHOR

People seem to be more interested in my name than where I get my ideas for my stories from. So I might as well share the story behind my name with all my readers.

My momma was born and raised in New Orleans. At the age of twenty, she met and fell in love with an Irishman named Patrick Riley Dwyer. Needless to say, the family was a bit taken aback by this as they hoped she would marry a family friend. It was a modern day arranged marriage kind of thing and my momma downright refused.

Being that my momma's families were descendants of the original English speaking Southerners, they wanted the family blood line to stay pure. They were wealthy and my father's family was poor.

Despite attempts by my grandpapa to make Patrick leave and destroy the love between them, my parents married. They recently celebrated their sixtieth wedding anniversary.

I am one of six children born to Patrick and Lynn Dwyer. I am a combination of both Irish and a true Southern belle. With a name like Dixie Lynn Dwyer it's no wonder why people are curious about my name.

Just as my parents had a love story of their own, I grew up intrigued by the lifestyles of others. My imagination as well as my need to stray from the straight and narrow made me into the woman I am today.

For all titles by Dixie Lynn Dwyer, please visit
www.bookstrand.com/dixie-lynn-dwyer

Siren Publishing, Inc.
www.SirenPublishing.com

Lightning Source UK Ltd.
Milton Keynes UK
UKHW02f1352160318
319572UK00006B/943/P